The Space Between

Gerry Turcotte

En Route Books and Media, LLC
Saint Louis, MO
USA

ENROUTE
Make the time

En Route Books and Media, LLC

5705 Rhodes Avenue

St. Louis, MO 63109

Contact us at

contactus@enroutebooksandmedia.com

Cover Credit: Sophie J. Turcotte

Copyright © 2026 Gerry Turcotte

ISBN-13: 979-8-88870-490-5

Library of Congress Control Number: 2026932362

The first chapter, 'My Career as an Altar boy,' originally appeared in *Flying in Silence*, published by Cormorant Books in Canada and Brandl and Schlesinger in Australia, 2001. 'Prayer and Medication' originally appeared as a column in *Small Things: Essays on Faith and Hope*, published by Novalis, 2016.

DEDICATION

FOR SOPHIE & GÉRARD

SOULMATES

"Truth lives in the spaces between words. It defies translation."

Ashok K. Banker

Thirty spokes meet in the hub,
But the empty space between them
Is the essence of the wheel

***

Walls with windows and doors
Form the house,
But the empty space within it
Is the essence of the home

Laozi

"How can I begin anything new with all of yesterday in me?"

Leonard Cohen, *Death of a Ladies' Man*

TABLE OF CONTENTS

Part One:

In which our hero devotes his life to the service of the Church...........1

Part Two:

In which our hero leaves the comfort of the known world behind ...59

Part Three:

In which our hero devotes his life to the service of women 129

Part Four:

In which our hero is tragically brought down to earth.................... 191

Afterword:

PART ONE

In which our hero dedicates his life to the service of the Church

One

MY CAREER AS AN ALTAR BOY

When I turned nine, I became an altar boy at the local church. I remember the lovely uniform I got to wear, and the exquisite smell of the incense in the change rooms. On my first day the priest, Fr. Rémi, explained that I would lead the procession out into the church, carrying the gold crucifix on a long silver pole. 'Hold it up proudly,' he said, but he forgot to warn me about the low archway.

I was demoted to bell ringer. 'Don't worry,' he said, 'I'll tell you when you're meant to ring them.'

At the altar, during the most sacred ceremony on my first day of serving Mass, I looked out at the four people in the congregation. Two of these were my parents, who had fought their way through the worse snowstorm of the year to watch their son's great triumph. They were smiling up at me, waving surreptitiously. I was about to wave back when I felt the priest's foot poking me in the ribs.

I looked up at him and he stood with the oversized host raised in his hands. He was looking up towards the ceiling, but his mouth was angled down.

'Now, boy. Ring the bell.' I started ringing for my life. The sound was magical. It reminded me of Christmas — of sleigh bells. I lowered my head and shut my eyes so tightly that I actually saw stars. And I rang those bells. I thought to myself, 'No one will ever ring these as well or as loudly.'

The priest kicked me sharply in the ribs and knocked the breath out of me. 'For goodness sake, knock it off!' he said.

I stared up at him through watery eyes. 'But you said....' I began.

'Shh!' he whispered, slipping briefly into Latin, and then, correcting himself, repeating the words in English.

He nudged me again, gently this time, and I let forth with another tremendous ring of the bells that he cut short with such a sharp jab of his foot that I let out a yell. Make up your mind, I thought angrily!

Later, because of my unfamiliarity with the vestments, I found that I was the last one in the change room. The priest seemed pleased to find me there. He moved in and poked his flushed face in my vicinity.

He seemed terribly uncomfortable. I watched his mouth, as he said, 'Well, that wasn't so bad,' and then only half understood as he explained that perhaps I wasn't cut out for this. Years later, when I thought about this time, I wondered insecurely if I was the only altar boy ever to be fired. At the time, though, I only felt relief.

Outside the church, in the blistery winter air, my mother hugged me tightly. She was crying.

'You were *so* good,' she said. 'I'm sure you could hear those bells all over town.'

Two

A LIFE OF SERVICE

Although I had failed spectacularly as an altar boy, I believed deep in my bones that I had a higher calling and knew there were many other ways to help the church. It took a while for me to figure out exactly what that would look like, but I'm happy to say that I eventually had a vision that set me on the right path. The volunteer who cleaned the church was in her nineties. To suggest that the job was beyond her would be like saying a nine-year-old boy was unlikely to be drafted into the NHL. My mother told me that the old lady saw it as her penance. Perhaps that's why it was so painful to watch.

If I couldn't be an altar boy, I decided I could help behind the scenes. I'd offered to do so before and Fr. Rémi, bless him, always asked — begged really — that I not help in any way, shape or form. That's how magnanimous he was. I knew that this was just his Christian way of modestly refusing help, so it was essential for me to ignore his protestations. Since he was clearly embarrassed about accepting assistance, however, I understood that whatever service I rendered had to be done discreetly.

The vision that I had one misty morning showed me how I could assist the beleaguered priest *and* the cleaning lady all in one fell swoop. My father had a hardware store, but in those days most of the products we sold were delivered to us in bulk — solvent, nails, bleach, potting soil — and it was often my job to transfer these into smaller packaging which we sold to the customers. Because of this, I knew that I could 'borrow' small amounts of these materials when I needed to do odd jobs, usually for school projects. I went into my dad's workshop and borrowed his electric drill, fitted it with an industrial buffer, and then grabbed a quart of wax and an extension cord. I waited until the cleaning lady had finished her shift and then let myself into the church, which in those days was never locked. The idea I had was to help restore all the incredible woodwork back to its original shine.

I decided to start with the first pews, which is where all the community VIPs always sat. I spread the wax over the wood in generous strokes and rubbed it in with a rough cloth. Then I plugged the drill in and began to polish it to a lustrous finish. It took longer than I expected, and I was completely exhausted by the time I got to the third row. It occurred to me that I didn't need to do all of them in one sitting. So instead, I headed towards Fr. Rémi's presider's chair. Like the pews, it was built from golden oak, though it had seen better days. I put my back into it and scrubbed and polished until the chair positively gleamed. Job well done, I thought.

I was so excited to see the reaction of the parishioners that I decided to attend the 7 am mass the next morning, something that was unusual for me to say the least. Frankly, I was usually lucky to get up in time for the 11 am service. Fr. Rémi, who stood at the back of the church greeting his flock, seemed similarly surprised to see me. I rushed past him and sat in the back pew, anxious to watch the reaction of the community as they came in and saw the gleaming wood. Unfortunately, the lights were dimmed, and so it didn't really pop as I'd hoped it would. Still, it was impossible for me to wipe the grin off my face, and I noticed that this seemed to be troubling Fr. Rémi who kept shooting glances my way. Of course, for once I had a clear conscience.

I watched as the neighbourhood big shots made their way towards the front pew. They donated the most to the church, though I only knew this because they reminded us at every opportunity. Their gift entitled them, apparently, to exclusive use of the front row. I'm sure if they could have had a seat next to the altar, they would have claimed it. In any event, I watched as Mrs. Maugière sat first, giving herself a slight push to the side to make room for her husband. To her surprise — and mine too if I'm honest — she shot along the pew like a puck on ice. She let out a 'waaah!' noise that only stopped when she struck the end of the row with a muffled thud.

Her husband was already in the process of seating himself when his wife whisked away and in an effort to reach out and grab her, he somehow projected himself along the seat as well. He, like his wife, let out a strange 'weeeh' sound, though perhaps an octave lower. I could see him careening towards her and the image of a bowling ball came to mind. I looked away to avoid seeing the collision, though the 'ooomph' sound they made was surprisingly harmonized.

I considered myself a person of above average intelligence, and even at such a young age I had already read one or two Sherlock Holmes stories, so I was familiar with the concept of logical deduction. So, when other parishioners, each in their turn began slipping up and down the first three pews like frozen fish sticks I began to suspect it might have something to do with the wax I'd applied so diligently. Perhaps I had overdone it with the buffer, I thought, though there could be no question that the wood positively gleamed.

In the meantime, Fr. Rémi had greeted everyone and left to prepare for his entrance. The music began and those who could quickly stood. I watched begrudgingly as some kid I didn't know carried the cross in ahead of Fr. Rémi, who made his way up to the altar, bowed and then moved to his seat. He began his greeting, but I no longer heard what he was saying. It occurred to me suddenly that I had spent twice as much time polishing his beautiful throne, as I liked to call it, and I thought it was absolutely essential that someone warn Fr. Rémi of the potential for catastrophe that awaited. When I say someone, I wasn't exactly sure who else could do this, but to be fair, I was in the very last row, and just a small person with a tiny voice. What, in the Lord's name, could I possibly do? So I of course did nothing.

Fr. Rémi blessed everyone and invited us to be seated. And then I heard a whoop and saw him disappear over the edge of his seat. I must have put too much wax because once he hit the ground he just kept going. I'm not sure where he landed because it occurred to me then and there that I should get a start on my homework and departed without looking behind me. Like Fr. Rémi, the parishioners also tried to regain their seats. Swear words in French are all religious, and I was surprised to hear the many creative ways the Lord's name could be taken in vain as I fled the church. I will say this, however, the smell of the wax was absolutely heavenly, and that, surely, had to count for something.

Three

THE NATIVITY SCENE

When I volunteered to help set up the church's nativity scene Fr. Rémi wept. I am sure that he simply couldn't believe his luck, or how generous I was. When he said, 'Please, anything but that,' I knew in my heart of hearts that it was a plea to do more. And how could I say no? He was no longer on crutches from when he slipped off his presider's chair, and he seemed to have newfound energy. But the nativity scene was a complex creation, housed in the bowels of the church, which was resurrected every December, usually using paint, lumber and additional bits and pieces that my father somewhat reluctantly provided. It seemed only fair that I help as well.

Christmas was one of the parish's busiest times and Fr. Rémi was run off his feet preparing for the week of sacred festivities. He had choirs to manage, homilies to write, volunteer events to coordinate. The nativity scene was the one thing that he sub-contracted out to the community and that could go ahead without him. It was also true to say that the same group of people took charge every year, so there was a certainty about the project and its execution. Michoo and Léon were both carpenters, and they knew how to assemble the complex jigsaw puzzle, but they still needed plenty of hands to unpack the boxes, fetch new straw and paint, and to help position the motley collection of life-sized statues that we had acquired over the years.

As one might expect, parishioners had provided oddly sized creatures for the crèche. There was a gigantic lamb that looked as though it had survived countless rodeos, and a beat-up bull that appeared to have lost at just as many. There was a donkey that resembled a two-person costume, crudely sewn together. Someone had provided a rather lovely emu, complete with lifelike feathers, and for whatever reason it was included every year. The three wise men, admittedly, looked more like the three stooges, but if you squinted it wasn't so bad. More importantly, the community had rallied together to acquire reasonable representations of the Holy Family. That, at least, was a relief.

In the days leading up to Christmas we assembled in the parish hall and slowly put all the pieces side by side. That way we were able to identify what was missing, what needed to be repaired and repainted, and what had to be replaced. I was pleased to see that the carpenters treated me like an equal, and I spent a few nights repainting the manger, fitting the crib together and then sourcing a roughhewn blanket that would be used to cover the baby Jesus, all without supervision.

The winter was brutal, but we used a break in the weather to shovel a space clear of snow where we erected the nativity scene. We'd chosen a spot that was near the ground lights, so the scene seemed deliberately and expertly lit. The finishing touch was to put the figures in place, which we did with care and reverence. To Fr. Rémi's apparent surprise, the carpenters praised my work and thanked me for my diligence. As a kid it felt good to be acknowledged in this way. Father kept pointing at me and saying, 'Him?', which I took to mean he wanted them to praise me over and over. What a great guy. In fact, the nativity scene worked out so well that Fr. Rémi decided he would build it into the Midnight Mass, with an invitation at the end of the service for everyone to follow him out into the snow, where he would offer a special prayer for the birth of Jesus. Our little choir would then sing 'The First Noël.'

Our apartment was directly across the street from the church. Usually this was an inconvenience. The parishioners often looked up at my room on Sundays and if they saw me made hand gestures telling me to get to Mass. And of course, the hourly bells made it impossible to sleep in. But at Christmas, with the church lit spectacularly, it was rather magical. And this year I got to look out my window at the nativity scene that I had helped to build.

Two days before Christmas, or Christmas Eve-Eve as we jokingly called it (well okay, only me), I was looking out my window and saw a group of kids fussing around the nativity scene. They were acting suspiciously, and they left carrying a large garbage bag. I feared the worse, and I made my way down the stairs and across the street to investigate. At first, I couldn't see what they'd done, but as I worked my way across the scene, I noticed that the crib was empty. They'd stolen the baby Jesus.

I was so incensed that I wanted to scream. The statue we had was one of the few that was beautifully made. There was no way the crib could be left empty. What would Fr. Rémi say if he arrived after Mass to bless the exhibit and found the baby gone? He would be heartbroken. I ran back to my room and ransacked my closet. All I had was a large stuffed creature that I'd won at a summer fair. It was supposed to represent a superhero of some kind but done so poorly it was impossible to know who it was meant to be. The size, though, was perfect. I pulled all the cartoonish insignias off it and drew a wide smile on its face with my red marker. In the morning I snuck down to the nativity scene and put the replacement in, covering the figure as much as I could with blankets.

Later that day I walked past to check my handy work and saw that the kids had stolen the replacement as well. I was furious but I would not be defeated. I ran back to my room and cobbled together another baby. I waited until one of the early masses had started and snuck back down. I replaced the baby Jesus for a second time. I kept a close eye on the installation after that, but there was only so much I could do.

That evening, as I prepared to attend the Midnight Mass, I snuck over first to make sure everything was in order. The stuffed white rabbit that I had altered was still there. I'd tweaked the ears so that they looked somewhat like a halo. All was well. I headed home and then crossed over with my folks at the appropriate time. My parents knew that I had played a role in building the nativity scene, so when I told them I was heading out just ahead of Fr. Rémi to get a good vantage point, they completely understood. When mass ended, Fr. Rémi began to move with the congregation towards the door, and I slipped out first. I reached the scene only to discover that baby Jesus had once again been stolen.

There was no time to return to the apartment. I could see the congregation heading towards the stairs, led by Fr. Rémi. How could he bless the scene if Jesus wasn't there? I didn't know what to

do. I was panicking. All our work was for nothing. And then I remembered: I had assembled the crib. I knew how it was configured.
Without a second thought I crawled under the little structure and
wriggled into the space where our baby Jesus statue had been. Half
my body stuck out beyond the crib but was hidden by straw. I
pulled the blankets up to my chin and tried to disappear into the
background as much as possible and went deathly still.

No sooner was I in position than I heard Fr. Rémi approach.
He had the large thurible in his hand, which I hadn't expected, and
the incense was wafting thickly all around me. He began to pray.
Halfway through he paused. He was staring hard at the crib. At me.
It was difficult for me to stay still, and I felt a sneeze coming on. He
leaned in so close that our eyes, perhaps inevitably, met. 'Hi,' I said.
Then I sneezed. I'd never heard Fr. Rémi scream before, and for an
older man he ran incredibly quickly. The parishioners fell back too,
some to their knees, but most running back into the church. I tried
to wriggle out to explain but I was stuck fast. As I struggled to get
free a face came into view. 'Hi Dad!'

My father looked at me quizzically. 'I thought that was you,' he
said. 'I'd know that sneeze anywhere.' He paused, glanced over to
the church and then back at me. 'Do I want to know?' he asked.

My mother's face appeared beside his. 'Son?'

'I can explain,' I pleaded. 'This is not as bad as it looks.'

My father sighed. 'When you were born the doctors said you
were a miracle birth, but I don't think this is what they meant. Let's
get you out of there.'

By the time I was extracted the word had spread, and when I
was finally pulled free, we headed toward the church. I saw Fr. Ré-

mi framed by the interior lights. His silhouette, I must say, was ominous. As we walked towards him, he held up his hand. He pointed towards our apartment. My father patted me on the shoulder. 'Too soon. We'll have a chat with him tomorrow.'

We turned towards our house. 'Dad?' I said sheepishly. He looked down at me kindly. 'Merry Christmas.'

'Indeed,' he answered, smiling as always. 'My little Christmas miracle.'

Four

THE GREAT SCHISM

It goes without saying that I was an incredibly wise ten-year-old child. Everyone thought so. I made sure of it. And because I bore the burden of being the intellectual in our gang, I took it upon myself to bring great nuggets of wisdom to the community. There was no internet back then, but I had a battered, second-hand copy of one volume of the *Encyclopedia Britannica*, so it was only right that I bring knowledge to my people. Especially since I was the only one who could read English, widely believed to hold the answers to many of the world's great mysteries.

To put this superior mindset into context, I once helped to preserve the Catholic faith among the youth of my small corner of working-class Montreal, averting what I was sure would have been a major exodus. At a gathering of our five-person gang, my friend J.P. announced that he would be leaving the Church, never to return.

'It has no connection to my life. Everything is set in the olden times in foreign places. What's the point?'

Nodding wisely, I demonstrated both patience and magnanimity as I gently set him straight. 'That's not quite true. Many of the most important events in the Bible happened in Canada.' There was a moment of stunned silence shattered by a chorus of disagreement. Finally, Laurence, the only girl that was permitted in our gang, threw down the gauntlet: 'Give me one example.'

That was the moment I was waiting for. 'Everyone knows that Jesus was crucified in Calgary. It's in the Gospels.' To say that my triumph was sweet is an understatement. Everyone turned to look at J.P.

'He's got you there, bud,' Laurence chirped.

J.P. rarely conceded a point, but this was bigger than all of us. 'Well,' he agreed, 'that changes things. I guess I'll give the church another chance.' Laurence looked at me admiringly.

'It's the least I can do for ectoplasmic harmony.'

'What's that?' she asked, growing more impressed by the minute.

'That's when different religions work together.' The gang members were nodding now. Something important had happened though we didn't quite grasp it.

'Wow,' Réal, the youngest member finally said. 'All this time I thought they only did the stampede in Calgary.'

'The world is more complicated than any of us can imagine,' I said sagely. 'Anyone want to get a soda?'

And that was how I saved the church from possible extinction in my small neighbourhood. You're welcome.

Well, to a point, the above is true. For a time. The great schism, as it came to be called, admittedly only by me, occurred a few months later. Order in the faith had been restored by yours truly and everyone in my gang was missing only three or four masses a month (a record for sure), and all of our souls seemed decidedly more robust, when a tragic event disrupted our now deeply Catholic gang. J.P. fell in love with a girl who was Precipriterian. We weren't quite sure what that meant, but it sounded terrible, and my best friend was frankly devastated. Catholics frowned upon marriages with Precipriterians, and my ten-year-old friend was crushed.

I knew first-hand how monumental this type of situation could be. When my mother converted to Catholicism to marry my father an article ran in the local gazette announcing that he had heroically saved her soul by marrying her. My Aunt Philomène never quite forgave him for publicly shaming the family, even heroically. But at least my mother wasn't Precipriterian — she was just Protesting. My best friend's situation seemed decidedly worse. She wore a cross, but she had kicked Jesus right off it.

'Did you explain that Jesus was crucified in Calgary and everything?' I asked, wanting to be helpful.

'We didn't get into religion,' J.P. admitted miserably, 'I was too busy trying to kiss her.'

His younger brother, eavesdropping, shuddered. 'That's gross,' he shouted. 'You'll get spit all over your lips.'

J.P. nodded, clearly in agreement. 'I know, but it's what a man of the world has to do. Otherwise we can't get married.'

'You can't anyway,' I added forcefully.

'Because I'm only ten?' J.P. asked.

'No, stupid, because she's Precipriterian.'

'But I'm *also* only ten.'

'Okay,' I conceded, 'but one problem at a time. First we have to overthrow her religion.'

'Not sure how that's possible,' J.P. muttered, more miserable now than ever, and I admit I was somewhat offended at his lack of faith in me.

'Perhaps if we go over to their church and explain how they've got things wrong,' I suggested. 'Tell them about Calgary. You were ready to abandon the church before I explained it to you.'

J.P. nodded eagerly. A glimmer of hope was dawning. 'It's possible. I'm sure there are worse ideas.' Looking back on it now, it's hard to imagine how that could possibly be true. But at the time a feeling of relief began to grow in all of us. If I'd saved religion once, why couldn't I do it again? At this rate, I thought, I would be cannonballed by the church in no time. I might even get my own medallion.

So that's how I ended up in a local church that I had never visited before. I wasn't sure if it was the same Precipriterian one that J.P.'s true love attended, but it had unfamiliar markings on the door, and no crucifix anywhere in sight. I walked towards a young man at the entrance and came right out and asked: 'Could I see the boss, please?'

The kid looked at me with an odd expression on his face, but then shrugged his shoulders. 'The rabbi's right over there.'

'Okey-dokey,' I said. How hard can this be? I thought.

I'm disappointed to admit that my theological foray into the opposite camp was not as successful as I'd hoped it would be, but I did get a free cup of tea and a pastry that I hadn't ever seen before. The boss priest was very nice, but he spent most of his time doubled over laughing as I explained the basics of theological thought, telling me that he couldn't be all that serious. Part of me was insulted, but the pastry kind of made it all worth it. In the end, as he walked me out, the elderly gentleman very kindly agreed to think through my arguments and promised to let me know if he had a change of heart. Honestly, I knew that it was unlikely, and several weeks later I noticed that none of the signage on the building had changed, so I guessed that my argument wasn't as convincing as I'd hoped. Still, there was the chance that our conversation would be reported and perhaps even reach the young lady who had started the great schism in the first place.

When I caught up with J.P. a few days later I felt hopeful. 'Well, I've started the ball rolling,' I assured him. 'I've spoken to the powers that be. Hopefully the word will get around and the girl will have a change of heart. She might yet see the light.'

J.P. looked at me, confused. 'What girl?' he asked.

'The Precipriterian. The one you want to marry.'

'Oh her,' he said. 'It's okay. I'm way too young to settle down. Mom says I should be fishing in the sea first, whatever that means.'

And with that, order was restored. I had done what I could to bring stability to the church. Now all I had to do was wait to be cannonballed by the pope. I said the word out loud: Saint. It had a nice ring to it.

Five

STALAG

It is not at all well known about me that I was an action hero long before it was popular to identify as one. At least I thought so. A look back at my rather remarkable youth shows that I was an adventurous, debonair child who had little by way of phobias or fears — other than a profound discomfort around women, death, snakes, sushi, water, gravel, playgrounds, origami, and a few other odds and ends. Perhaps because of this, friends often turned to me to take care of pressing matters. 'The building's on fire. He'll go in and get your backpack,' or, 'You dropped your keys in the lake. He'll jump in and find them.' And other loving and supportive moments like that, which could have happened, had fires or water been a part of my life. Just because none of this had actually happened didn't mean it couldn't.

So, it should come as no surprise to anyone that when a major crisis occurred one blistery winter night, that yours truly saved the day. Yes, again. Winter had set in, and although we had been warned, the snowstorm that descended on the city was catastrophically paralyzing. Even the incredible snow removal infrastructure of Montreal was defeated, and volumes of snow descended on the city in a matter of hours, and then for good measure continued throughout the night. We awoke to a winter wonderland, where traffic had disappeared and only snow mobiles zigzagged up and down otherwise preternaturally quiet streets.

My father and I stood at my bedroom window in the tiny second floor apartment above his store. My room looked out onto the main street, which was invisible beneath mountains of snow. 'Well, I guess I'm having a snow day,' I announced, using a voice that feigned disappointment and boredom all at once.

My dad snorted. 'You kidding? It's just a dusting. Get your boots.' My dad did not shut down for anyone. I reluctantly got dressed, pulled on a tattered pair of ski pants and my winter boots, packed my lunch and headed down the stairwell to the front door. When I opened it the entrance was completely blocked by a snowdrift.

'Ah Dad, I think we have a problem.' It occurred to me, of course, that this was also an opportunity. If I climbed to the top of the stairs and then ran down as fast as I could, I'd be able to plunge through the doorway into oblivion. It was certainly an intoxicating plan. I climbed quickly to the top of the stairs, and just as I was preparing to run down my father grabbed my coat.

'Don't!' he said. 'Looks fun, but all the snow will pour in. Everything will be soaked. Close up and meet me in your room.'

I was crestfallen for sure, but there was also a glimmer of hope that I'd be let off from school. I quickly shut the door and made my way back upstairs. 'Son, what we have here is an opportunity.' I nodded vigorously. Indeed. TV, early morning cartoons, classes cancelled. Life was good.

'I've always wanted to know,' he continued, 'if we could jump from the roof into the snowbank below,' he said. I looked up at him with what was no doubt a puzzled expression. He looked down at me. 'Don't tell me you've never thought about it?'

I shook my head. 'No. Never. Why would I?'

My father's head was nodding. 'Exactly. Why shouldn't we?'

I began to object. 'That's not what I said.'

He turned to face me with a look of manufactured shock. 'How is this any different to you jumping off the roof into the pool?' he asked. Now I was really confused. We had a rickety above ground pool that was barely three feet deep in the back yard which I may or may not have jumped into from the roof. 'But you told me to stop doing that and grounded me.' He would brook no opposition.

'Exactly. You only live once.'

My father had an annoying habit of starting a conversation mid-way into it, as though we'd been discussing something for hours. When that happened the best thing was to run as quickly as you could to catch up with his train of thought. 'So if there was ever a fire, we need to know we can escape safely.'

'We have a fire escape,' I added helpfully.

'What if it catches fire?'

'It's cast iron.'

My father looked genuinely hurt. 'So you would want us to perish in a fire?' he said. I was shaking my head. No of course not. 'Your poor mother would be a widow.'

'Not if she was in the fire too,' I offered helpfully. The look on his face told me that he was deeply disappointed in me but still willing to let me make it up to him. I couldn't let him down.

'Help me to pry the window open,' he said, and with that we struggled with the frozen frame until it was open wide enough to let me through. My father looked at me seriously. 'You're doing this for the family. Remember that. We're proud of you.' I nodded seriously. I was beginning to get excited about this. Usually when I came up with incredibly dangerous and stupid ideas my father talked me out of them. This time he had only himself to blame if I got impaled on a fence post and bled to death in the blindingly white snow. There was so much to look forward to.

'You can count on me,' I said, pausing to salute. He saluted back, confused for a moment, and then handed me a shovel.

'Once you're down there make sure to clear the doorway of the store and the apartment. And then head off to school.' I was about to wriggle through the opening, but my dad stopped me with his hand. 'Your country thanks you.' We were getting into the spirit of this. I liked it.

'It's the least I can do.' I wriggled into the narrow opening just in time to hear my mother shriek behind me.

'Don't you dare,' I heard her say, so I pulled myself the rest of the way and headed as quickly as I could to the edge of the building. Now that I had built up my hopes for the adventure, I wanted to make sure nothing got in my way. I heard my father say, half-heartedly, 'Don't do it, son, what was I thinking,' in the mock-heroic voice he would sometimes use when we were messing around. It translated to: 'Go get 'em tiger!'

Perched on the edge of the roof and looking down into the white abyss of the snow, I felt a sudden surge of adrenaline. A lesser man would call it sheer panic. This was living I thought. I scanned the surrounding landscape. The streets were deserted. The wind was whipping off the snow and causing small whirlwinds of crystal dust everywhere. It was a magical morning. I thought of all the action heroes I had watched growing up. I summoned the ghost of Steve McQueen in *The Great Escape*, about to drive his motorcycle into the barbed wire in an attempt to escape Stalag Luft III. I was one step away from becoming just like him. I looked back at my parents who were staring at me through the windowpane. My dad had a goofy expression, mocking my imminent death. My mother was using every muscle in hers to make clear that she would kill me if I died. What to do, what to do? I thought. And then, holding the shovel above my head, like a marine holding his weapon above the water, I stepped off the roof. I landed softly in the snowbank two feet below and sank to my waist.

You could enter the store from a trapdoor in the floor that my father had made to avoid having to go outside in bad weather. I realized immediately that he'd already checked things out and knew the snow pretty much reached the roofline. I hadn't been at risk in any way. Admittedly, that took the shine off things. He just needed me to clear the snow from the front entrance. Snow which I felt was melting into my waistband. I lowered my arms and struggled to get free. I was stuck solid. I heard crunching, and when I looked over, there was our elderly neighbour walking his dog.

'What are you doing there?' he asked as his cocker spaniel yipped at me.

'Saving my parents,' I answered seriously. 'They're stuck in the house, starving. I have to get them out.'

My neighbour nodded his head. 'Good boy,' he chirped, and the dog wagged its tail, thinking the compliment was meant for him. Without sparing me a second thought he moved on. I struggled some more, feeling the cold seeping into my joints. I wondered briefly if I would need to chew off a limb if I didn't break free. I supposed I could drink my own urine if needs be. The world really was enchanting and filled with possibility. Despite the excitement of death and dismemberment, I allowed myself a moment of self-pity, imagining the pain of frost bite. My groin, I realized, was most at risk, sitting well beneath the snow. That concentrated my mind. I refused to compromise my masculinity in this way.

And so, with the seriousness of a true hero, I began the laborious work of shoveling myself out of the snowbank, clearing the doorways, and restoring order to the chaos. When I was done, almost as though it were choreographed by a Hollywood director, both the doors to the store and the apartment whipped open simultaneously. My mother, furious, stood in one, my father, beaming, in the other. 'You're grounded!' shot out from her lips just as 'Great job!' emerged from his. I looked from one to the other and then planted the shovel in the snowbank.

'But I'm late for school,' I announced matter-of-factly, and shrugged innocently. My mother paused, fuming, and then slammed the door. I looked at my dad. He winked back at me and saluted.

'Better get going, soldier', he said, 'People might need saving at the school too.'

I saluted. 'Yes sir!' I said and headed off into the winter wilderness to save the day. Steve McQueen had nothing on me.

Six

THE MUSIC OF THE SPHERES

I was never the type of kid who felt he knew everything, but I was reasonably certain that I was an authority on music. I'd heard the opening bars of Bach's 'Toccata and Fugue', so I felt I had classical music covered, and I knew *Madame Butterfly* wasn't an insect, so I had opera in the bag. I have to confess, however, that I was pleasantly, though suspiciously pleased, when Fr. Rémi, approached me one Sunday after Mass and asked for my advice. He was keen to find a way to make the service more appealing to young people, he said, and thought that as a particularly wise and inspiring young man that I might be able to help him. Well, what he actually said was, 'You're young. What do you think?' In my book that meant the same thing.

So, once I was certain that he hadn't mistaken me for someone else, I suggested that the music could be more contemporary. Fr. Rémi agreed that it could be a good experiment for the midday Mass. I knew I was flirting with heresy, but I pushed the envelope. 'Perhaps an electric guitar or two,' I suggested helpfully. It is important to understand how staid the local parish was. A triangle and a mouth organ would have seemed high tech. So guitars... To my surprise though, Fr. Rémi nodded. Well, his head moved in a way that was not specifically a no.

I was part of a garage band at the time — The Green Boogers — and I knew it would be inappropriate to volunteer myself, but my two best friends were ripe for the picking. And if it worked, I could then join them on stage at a later date. I took a chance: 'As it happens, Father, I know just the group. J.P. and Réal specialize in sophisticated contemporary music. More importantly,' I added wisely, 'they speak the language of today's youth.' I left out the fact that we had never performed in public and had only taught ourselves how to play guitar a few months earlier. Still, I thought, how hard could it be? And parishioners were ordered to be charitable. It was in every single sermon. I was quite sure they could be excommunicated if they criticized us. Fr. Rémi looked dubious, but he was also keen to get more young people in the door.

'J.P. and Réal would love to do this,' I assured him.

'Do they even come to church?' Fr. Rémi asked, struggling to remember the kids that lived next door.

'Are you kidding? They're the most saintly people I know!'

'Are you out of your mind?' J.P. shouted when I told him he'd been booked to perform the following Sunday. J.P. hadn't set foot inside the church in a full year, ever since he got kicked out for falling asleep in the confessional. That and his Precipriterian crisis as we knowledgeably called it.

'You'll be great,' I assured him. 'Everybody in the neighbourhood knows you, and they're all devout Christians. They *have* to be charitable. It's the law. Or they go to puberty.' I think I meant purgatory, but I hadn't read Dante at that stage.

My extraordinary reasoning was having an effect, but I could tell he still wasn't fully convinced. 'Plus, the ladies from the all-girl Catholic school will be there. They're all unmarried.'

'Course they are, stupid. They're twelve.'

'Still single,' I repeated sagely.

J.P.'s head was nodding. 'And girls love the bad boy. I'll do it.'

I wish I could say that the week was packed with diligent rehearsing, but the truth is we then all promptly forgot about it until the following Saturday. It was Réal who reminded us. 'Aren't we supposed to be doing something tomorrow?'

'Oh my God, you're right,' J.P. said, 'I told my cousin I'd go bowling with him.'

'Cool,' I said. And then, because of my incredible intelligence and ability to plan I interjected: 'Crap! You're performing at the twelve o'clock Mass.'

'Whaaaat?' they said. 'I thought that was....' And then we paused, the reality of the crisis sinking in.

'J.P., you need to do this. Figure out a song that will be appropriate. There's a lot at stake here.' I was going to say something about his soul, but then I looked at my friend. I didn't think that would carry much weight. 'I'm pretty sure you get part of the collection money if you do a good job.'

His face went through what was a fascinating array of emotions, from angry to terrified to greedy and then, finally, resolved. 'I have just the song,' he said. I must confess I didn't like the newest expression on his face. He looked slyly at his younger brother. 'The one we tried last week.' My heart sank as Réal's neutral expression lit up. Something like what I'd imagine a demon's might do before he corrupted a human heart.

'It has to be appropriate,' I emphasized.

'It is, it is,' Réal chirped up. 'It's got biblical stuff in it and everything. Now, go so we can rehearse. You want this to be good, don't you?' I left feeling as though I'd just been sold swampland in Florida. But let's face it, what else could I do? I was just the impresario. They were the talent.

Come the day I sat in the slippery front pew for the first time in my life. I figured that I was, effectively, the band's manager, and so I wanted to show solidarity and support for my two friends who, I was quite certain, were about to be publicly humiliated in a way that would be difficult to capture in words.

Fr. Rémi, bless him, had printed up posters on a broken-down Gestetner that invited all young people to the 'Electric Mass', a phrase that conjured up public executions and an electric chair, which, in the end, wasn't far off from what actually happened. 'Today,' he announced before we got started, 'We are having a special treat, with J.P. and Réal playing an opening hymn.'

My friend J.P. had been busy checking out the unmarried twelve-year-olds and didn't quite realize when it was his time to perform. He and Réal fumbled awkwardly with their guitar cases and pulled them free. I'm not sure I expected the look on Fr. Rémi's face when the shiny red guitars came out of the cases, the words Black Sabbath scrawled across them in blood red gothic letters. He seemed more perturbed by the picture of the satanic creature beneath the lettering, blood dripping from sharpened fangs partially submerged into a baby's body. If he was going to say

something, the moment was lost when both boys plugged their guitars into the massive amplifiers they'd brought and the feedback
rippled through the atmosphere like a surgical knife. My fillings
were literally buzzing.

The parishioners, you could see, were quite simply … let's go
with terrified. Fr. Rémi began to raise his finger, but too late. J.P.'s
hand dropped down across the opening chords of AC/DC's 'High-
way to Hell,' but at a decibel level the heavy metal group would
never have dared explore, which is really saying something. The
sound exploded through the speaker system and then careened off
the echo-chamber of the church. The elderly couples in the front
row beside me were blown back in their seats. In fact, though it's
slightly unclear to me now because of the passing years, I think a
couple of the older folks were literally projected two pews back.

J.P.'s voice was perfectly suited to the agonizing yet sensitive
lyrics, his range, thanks to puberty, shifting between the octaves
unpredictably. It had a certain charm, I thought, though I confess I
couldn't actually hear a thing. My head was beginning to throb,
and I may even have been nursing the start of a nosebleed. And
then, after what felt like an eternity, the final chord was struck, and
the entire congregation sat there listening to the shock waves of the
dying chord pinging from corner to corner like a bullet ricocheting
off canyon walls.

Fr. Rémi approached the ambo, looking somewhat grey. I
think, truth be told and with the benefit of hindsight, he looked as
though he was going to pass out. We were all deaf from the sound,
none more so than Fr. Rémy who had been standing right next to
the amplifier, and so his first words were shouted out at us: 'MY

DEAR FRIENDS,' and then he just seemed to lose his train of thought. His chin was wobbling, and his body began to shake. But then, rather miraculously I thought, he seemed to compose himself, and a somewhat concerning rictus transformed his face. 'My friends, I think you will agree that was an experience like no other. One, dear God, that we will never repeat again. So, please, bow your heads in prayer. Lord knows these youngsters need our help.'

I wasn't an expert, but that seemed hopeful. I looked up at J.P. and Réal. I gave them the thumbs up. Réal smiled back. J.P., though, was busy wriggling his eyebrows in the direction of the all-girl school. To their credit, the ladies looked suitably impressed. Truly they were connoisseurs of the music of the spheres. Then I looked over at Fr. Rémi. The look he was directing at me was inscrutable. No, that's not true. It was very scrutable. I knew I would need to go to the church up the road for the next little while. Just until his taste in music matured. It isn't easy, I'm sure you'll agree, being so far ahead of one's time.

Seven

PRAYER AND MEDICATION

When Fr. Rémi allowed me back into his Church I could tell he felt terrible about being so hard on me. I was sitting sheepishly in the back row debating whether or not I would go to confession when he came in and saw me sitting there. He seemed conflicted to see me. 'You're not planning any music?' he asked and did something to his face that was somewhat terrifying — he tried to smile. The gesture clearly cost him, but I appreciated the effort. He looked around cagily, no doubt worried someone else might have seen it, and then sat down next to me.

'How did I know the electric guitars could blow the parish fuse box and cause a fire?' I mumbled miserably.

'Well,' he said, 'We needed to re-wire it anyway. And the paint on that wall was outdated. It all worked out for the best. I got a new kitchen out of it, so that's something, I suppose.' I wasn't sure why he was being so nice to me. Usually, he turned brusquely away whenever I came near, and now here he was making small talk. Friendly small talk. 'So,' he said after a long pause, 'your mother tells me that you are quite the writer. I've been thinking about re-vamping the Church bulletin, and I want to add a section for youth. Is this something you might be interested in helping with?'

I must admit, I was shocked. The Church bulletin was a bland two-page affair that was produced with an old Remington typewriter and printed on an even older Gestetner. The tattered paper and the barely legible script were what I was sure the Dead Sea Scrolls must be like. Anything I could do to breathe life into the weekly bulletin would be a Godsend. And I wanted to be a writer. There were surely over 1000 copies of the bulletin produced each week which I was certain would instantly make me a best-selling author. In Canada anyway. I gladly agreed.

I rushed home immediately and told my parents. My father, on hearing the news, hung his head. 'Oh, he's a clever one,' he said. 'He's after my new Gestetner.' My father's store was directly opposite the Church, and the priests over the years constantly badgered him for free product. Every church sign was painted using my dad's paints and materials; the lawn was cut using the store's mower; and the picket fence was replaced largely through my father's generosity. He had drawn the line, though, at producing the weekly bulletin on his state-of-the-art printer, a hand-cranked, self-inking behemoth of a machine that someone had given him to settle a bill. Now, however, Fr. Rémi had found a work-around, knowing that my dad could hardly refuse to help me.

The first two weeks of our new arrangement were exhilarating. Fr. Rémi delivered a smudged, typed copy of the bulletin, with a tiny rectangle on the back page that was for Youth News. Here I was tasked with adding some information that would appeal to my demographic. Usually this consisted of several lines announcing a tombola to raise funds for the local hockey team, or a recruitment drive for the Christmas choir. I had to write out what I planned to say, then type it on my dad's typewriter, and present it for review. Once it had been triple-checked, I got to type it directly on the page, and then prepare it for printing. As my father feared, it was only two weeks into my editorial assignment that Fr. Rémi asked if we could use my dad's Gestetner instead of the failing Church one, and after that I was basically tasked with printing them after school or late on a Saturday, all at my father's expense.

I got so good at setting up the bulletin that Fr. Rémi gave me increasing responsibility, allowing me to transcribe the daily readings, to list the parish events, and even, on one occasion, to add a drawing of a Nativity scene that I'd made. In fact, I got so skilled at organizing the newsletter, and Fr. Rémi was saving such a lot of money by having my dad cover all the costs, that he finally gave me *carte blanche* to prepare the holiday edition. He presented me with a list of key events that were coming up, the workshops the Church would be hosting, and the relevant school performances that we always celebrated. 'Check and triple check your spelling,' he said, but then promptly forgot all about me.

As a would-be author I knew that I had an opportunity to leave my mark on the bulletin. Everyone agreed that it was staid and stodgy, and I knew it would take very little to make it punchier. I scoured the notes and flyers we'd been given and chose the pieces that I thought would be of most interest. I carefully set the first page, which was pretty much unchanging week after week: the readings, a summary of the homily, a message about Mass times. Fr. Rémi popped by and proofed the first page. 'Flawless!' he said happily, and left me to my own devices: rarely, I should add, a good thing.

Page two, I knew instantly, was my moment to shine. I gathered all the pieces and put them together as artistically as I could. I immediately changed all of Fr. Rémi's stilted phrasing. I typed with a care I'd never exercised before, paying special attention to the layout, and then, throwing caution to the wind, set about printing up the entire run for the Sunday services. 1900 one-sided masterpieces, sorted, stapled and ready to be distributed. Fr. Rémi, rushing from a community emergency, dropped by quickly and almost wept in gratitude when he saw that everything was done. I was covered in ink, smiling from ear to ear, and my hands were blistered from turning the printing handle over 4000 times. Fr. Rémi was so impressed he didn't even bother to proof the finished work. He nodded his head and patted mine. 'Great job, boy. Great job! Get them over to the Church, yes?'

'Absolutely, Father.'

As I was loading the boxes into our old wheelbarrow, my dad came into the store. 'All done then?'

I proudly handed him a copy. 'This is the first one that I did completely by myself.'

He nodded appreciatively and scanned the bulletin. When he got to the second page he paused, read and then re-read it. 'Has Fr. Rémi seen this?' he asked.

'Of course. He said, "Great job" and jumped for joy.' I allowed myself some room for artistic license, which I felt sure I would be getting more of.

My father smiled. He rarely attended Mass but he grabbed his coat. 'I think I might pop by today,' he said, and I felt a warmth inside me growing. Fr. Rémi had spoken ominously about my father going to hell if he didn't start coming to Mass. It warmed my heart knowing I was saving my dad by helping him to rediscover his faith.

And so it was that I distributed the bulletin to all the parishioners as they came in and felt rather proud as Fr. Rémi acknowledged my excellent work over the loudspeaker. That was the last comment he got to make. Suddenly laughter erupted from the pews. I hadn't put in any cartoons or levity of any kind that I could think of, but there was definitely an interest in the bulletin that I'd rarely seen.

Under miscellaneous items I'd written: 'You are invited to a Low Self-Esteem Support Group. Please use the back door.' I also informed parishioners that the cost to attend the prayer and fasting conference included meals. My most helpful addition was a gentle reminder: 'Ladies, don't forget the rummage sale. It's a chance to get rid of those things not worth keeping around the house. Don't forget your husbands.'

Under school performance I proudly announced: 'The eighth-graders will be presenting Shakespeare's *Hamlet* in the Church basement Friday at 7 PM. The congregation is invited to attend this tragedy.' And in the final line I helpfully informed everyone that there was a potluck on Saturday, 'with prayer and medication to follow.'

In the end, a church bulletin is a prayer of sorts that carries intentions, hopes, requests, and instructions for how to move throughout our week. It is also a gift that one person, or a team, makes both for the specific church, but also for the faith more widely. Just as importantly, it is an act of hospitality — a letter reaching out to all and reminding us that we are a people united by faith and by community. Why I should have been fired for attempting to do just that was beyond me, but my father was thrilled.

'Did I save you?' I asked a few days later.

'Yes,' he said energetically. 'You saved me a small fortune.'

Eight

TRUE CONFESSIONS

One of the regular routines in school was when Fr. Rémi visited and 'administered' confession as we liked to put it. Occasionally, though, in the lead up to Holy Week, the school bussed us to the local parish where we stood in line to confess our sins in the imposing and ornate confessional box that was purposefully built for our vast community of sinners. I was fairly certain that from a practical if not a theological standpoint the exercise was misjudged, because the behaviour of the guys in our grade usually worsened on any excursion the school was foolish enough to allow. All that free time waiting to confess moved us further, rather than closer, to a fit and proper state to receive communion. Nevertheless, it was an annual ritual, and we all enthusiastically complied, knowing that otherwise we'd be studying algebra.

As it happened, I was able to line up with my best friend J.P., but also a couple of young ladies that were intriguing if only because they had recently moved to the school and the teacher had ominously introduced them as converts. I didn't think it meant nuns in training, but I wasn't one hundred percent sure, so I was briefly on my best behaviour. One of the girls, Chantal Olivier, seemed particularly uncomfortable with the situation. She had a sheet of handwritten notes which she was studying nervously. 'What if I fail?' she asked her friend, 'I've only done this a couple of times.'

'You can't fail,' I assured her, seizing the opportunity. 'It's not a test. It's a … a process.' She looked at me with such gratitude and relief that I felt it only fair to expand a little. 'In fact, though, you're in an incredible church to be doing this.' I looked around melodramatically and then lowered my voice. Everyone leaned in. 'One time,' I explained to my captive audience, 'I came down here early. I was the only one in the church, so I opened the door to the confessional, and I was blown away by what I saw!'

'What did you see?' the young lady asked. It was intoxicating, I must confess, to have such a rapt audience.

'Well, I opened the door only to find that one entire wall was lined with amazing scotches. Bottle after bottle of the most expensive liquor. On the other wall, to my surprise, there were shelves filled with expensive cigars, the illegal kind that are rolled on the thighs of Cuban women. The other wall was lined with incredible artwork, beautifully framed, depicting some of the world's most exotic locations. The chair and kneeler were oak and elaborately padded. A beautiful fragrance filled the air. I thought that I was in heaven! When Fr. Rémi showed up I said to him, 'Father, this is really amazing. This must surely be the most sophisticated parish in the city.' And Fr. Rémi stared at me with his steely eyes and said, "Whatever kid, now get out of there, you're on my side of the box."'

When I wrapped up my well-rehearsed joke I was somewhat disappointed that no one in my audience even cracked a smile. I knew it wasn't brilliantly funny but it certainly didn't deserve contempt, though that wasn't quite the look they were giving me. In fact, if anything, they appeared rather terrified. I quickly realized that they weren't even looking at me. I turned to follow their gaze and saw that Fr. Rémi was standing right behind me. 'Get in the box,' he scowled at me, 'but I tell you now. You're starting with twenty Hail Marys right off the bat!'

'That sounds bad,' I heard Chantal whisper.

'I never had to do more than eight,' my friend J.P. responded comfortingly. 'What a legend.'

I made my way somberly into the confessional knowing that this wouldn't go well unless I was proactive. I waited for Fr. Rémi to get settled. He slid the little door back from the latticed window.

'Father?' I asked sheepishly.

'What?'

'Can I have one of these cigars?'

'That's forty Hail Marys!' he barked. 'Go out now and get started. I'll hear your confession when the other kids are done.'

'So no to the cigar?' I pressed, throwing caution to the wind.

'*Sixty* Hail Marys,' he hissed, but I detected the hint of a laugh in his voice. I thought I would take the win, such as it was, and snuck away to do my pre-penance penance. This time, as I left the box, my three pals were grinning from ear to ear, leaning in expectantly.

'Better lose the smile,' I whispered melodramatically, 'he can see in the dark!'

Chantal came and sat next to me as soon as she finished her confession.

'Thanks,' she said. 'I was nervous as hell about going in, but you really helped. I hope you didn't get into too much trouble.'

I shrugged. 'I'm kind of always in trouble with Fr. Rémi. He says I was put on this earth to test him. It's good to have a purpose in life, I suppose.' She laughed at that and then leaned in close.

'I think I'm in more trouble now then I was before,' she said.

'What do you mean?'

'I didn't know what to say in there, so I made up a bunch of stuff. Do you think God will mind?'

'Depends on what you made up. He really frowns on murder.'

She was nodding seriously. 'I didn't go that far. This time. I didn't want to max out on my first go.'

'That was really wise.' The door to the confessional began to open so we both dropped to our knees. I'd finished my Hail Marys but figured I could add a few extra for good measure. Fr. Rémi came over to our pew and grabbed me by the ear.

'Let's go,' he said, and I followed him back. I knew better than to push my luck again, so I was on my best behaviour. I made my confession, added a few extra poignant but believable sins which I knew I might eventually commit, and then Father blessed and absolved me of my sins. As I was about to step out, I heard him say, 'And leave the cigar.'

In all the years I had known Fr. Rémi I had never heard him make a joke. 'Yes, Father. Never again.' I always left the confessional feeling lighter — freed somehow from whatever burden I might be carrying, real or imagined. But on this day I left with an

extra spring in my step. Perhaps Fr. Rémi liked me after all. A rec-
onciliation, perhaps? One could only hope.

Nine

THE GIFT OF TONGUES

Occasionally customers in my father's dilapidated store would praise me for my bilingualism. 'It's such a gift,' they would say, but then they would complain about the bloody English, the damned French, or all those incomprehensible migrants. Honestly, it was incredibly confusing. What seemed, on the surface, to be a gift, kept proving itself to be a curse. The more languages you spoke, it seemed, the more opportunity to be misunderstood by a greater number of people. Or, as often happened in my neighbourhood, you were accused of being a member of an opposing faction just for speaking the language, which meant that you were an undesirable to everyone.

Sometimes clarity wasn't always welcomed. My cranky Aunt Philomène, for example, had always loved to go to Church. But when the New Mass came in, she initially freaked out. At first, she thought she had the gift of tongues and my father had to talk her out of her delusion. 'No, Sis, you don't have a miraculous gift. The priest is just saying the Mass in French instead of Latin.'

Even ten years after the change she continued to be incensed. 'I don't like it. I used to be able to tune out and never worried about what was said. I assumed it was really magical stuff. But now the words keep intruding on my "me" time, and it's all so ordinary. I would complain to Fr. Rémy but he's losing it.'

'Why is he losing it?' my father asked, and I could tell that he immediately regretted asking.

'The doddery old fool keeps facing the wrong way at the altar.'

I started to explain that this was also part of the New Mass, but my father raised his hand and did a discrete cutting gesture at his neck. I decided to leave the issue alone. He was right. No good could come of it.

To be fair, confusion reigned at home as well. My mother didn't speak French and my father didn't speak English when they met, and it wasn't until they had a child that they made an effort to learn the other's language. That might not seem significant except that they courted for eleven years. There were advantages to their imperfect grasp of their loved one's lingua franca. For one thing, when they were really upset, they tended to speak too quickly for the other to follow and so yours truly was called on to translate. One might think that this was a poisoned chalice, but I was a born diplomat. I sprinkled my translations liberally with flattery putatively from one to the other so that their arguments rarely lasted long.

'Dad says it's hard being mad at you because you have such beautiful eyes, even though he disagrees a tiny bit with your point of view.' And then, the other way: 'Mom says she can't really concentrate because you're so manly, but she was really hurt by what you said.' I usually had to leave the room within minutes because they'd be busy smooching and making up. It was, frankly, disgusting.

As a result of our linguistically confusing situation franglais became the paternal language of the household. Everyone spoke a mishmash of French-English. Unilingual friends were positively adrift. They would listen attentively, start to smile because they thought they grasped an idea, and then stare vacantly as it escaped into gibberish. 'Did you want a ... porcupine?' someone might ask at the table and my father would look at me concerned. 'What the hell is wrong with your friend?'

It was worse when friends made an effort to be understood. J.P., bless him, was frustrated by his inability to grasp English and so he always tried to engage my mother in conversation. 'You have nice nostrils,' he once said, 'And eyes two on your visage.' My mother nodded and turned towards me, a smile frozen on her face. 'Is your friend high?' she asked, and I was shocked that she even knew what that was. Actually, I didn't really know what that meant.

'No,' I answered helpfully. 'He's four foot eight.'

Because of the volatility of language, I learned to disguise my accent, which I could do effectively if I wasn't nervous. This meant that there were times where I might be at an event and a group of francophones would be attacking anglophones and I could just pretend to be unaffected and get out unscathed. More interesting would be when a group assumed I didn't speak their language and so would criticize me to one another. This happened once in a restaurant where the waiters assumed my family couldn't understand English. Throughout the meal they made patronising comments about us while smiling in our faces, which I translated for my dad. At the end, though, as we were paying the bill, I was delighted to address them in perfect, unaccented English, and to tell them exactly what I thought of them. My father smiled all the way home after that one. 'The looks on their faces,' he said. 'And yet they still asked for a tip.'

There were times, though, when I knew the issue cut deep. My father had grown up when it was a liability to be French and he had spent decades being discriminated against in the workforce because he couldn't speak English. The tide was turning in the language wars, but it didn't change the humiliation he had felt as a young man, fired for not being fluent, or told he could never be promoted. 'What would it look like,' one of his bosses had said to him, 'if a Frenchie became a manager. The company would be a laughingstock.' That was the last straw for him. It drove him out to the most remote parts of the city where he managed to buy a scrap of land and decided he would work for himself. The little shed of a hardware store that emerged in the empty field was in fact a monument of extraordinary confidence — a battle cry for a proud man who wouldn't be defined by prejudice.

'So how did you meet mom way out here?' I asked him once.

'Her dad, your grandfather, was a Scottish immigrant. He was even poorer than my family, which is saying a lot. This was the only place he could find that he could afford. And he worked for the telephone company.'

There were three buildings in the area around my father's property. One was the Church, built to cater to the migrants who worked in the factories along the train tracks nearby. The other was a beast of a telephone exchange that housed the Bell telecommunications company. The third was a *Dépanneur* — the ubiquitous convenience store that sold everything from newspapers to confection. Small rickety apartment blocks were sprinkled all around. My dad's hardware store was plumb in the middle of everything, an exclamation mark in an empty field. Unbeknownst to my dad at the time, the neighbourhood would grow rapidly, and to his shock he would find himself at the centre of it all.

Perhaps because of this, and much to my father's dismay, the store became a community hub of sorts, which meant that customers dropped in to socialize. This meant that my father couldn't just relax, or do his work, he had to be present while the different clients staked their claim. The Italians adored my dad because he had helped them when they first arrived. Many, in the early days, and to my mother's infinite distress, often paid their bills in kind: with a hastily plucked chicken or a recently carved leg of lamb. She drew the line at skinned rabbits which were surprisingly plentiful.

The Haitian clients who worked at the nearby factory, loved my dad because they could speak French together, and they often paid their bills with intriguing desserts. Some of the women, especially, confessed to my father that they had abandoned their families to help provide for them and send money home. My father, ever the soft touch, would accidentally forget to charge for items in their basket. 'To help them out,' he offered once when I tried to point it out. 'Don't say anything. That was me not so long ago.' That's us now, I wanted to add, but it seemed mean-spirited to say.

The curse of language became a gift of tongues one day though when a customer had what seemed like a fit in the store. The paramedics who arrived only spoke English, my father at the time mostly spoke French, and no one was quite sure what language the young man was speaking. My Aunt Philomène was visiting that day and her shrill cry called to me upstairs in the living room. I rushed down to see what the commotion was. 'They need you to translate,' she hissed angrily, 'The guy's speaking in tongues. I think he's possessed.'

I wanted to ask her why she thought I was the perfect candidate to help in that situation, but one of the paramedics saw me and called me over. 'He won't let us near him,' he said, and I could see the young man clutching his chest. 'You're young. Maybe he'll listen to you?' He was pressed back into the corner of the window display and was shouting incomprehensively, kicking his feet violently to keep everyone away. He was clearly in pain.

I wasn't sure, at first, how anyone thought I could help, but then I noticed his hands. I realized that he was signing. By pure chance, one of my classmates, whose brother was deaf, regularly taught us basic signs. I struggled to remember, and then slowly signed the words that I knew, hoping he spoke the same signing language. 'Friend,' I tried to say, 'Kind.' He looked at me suspiciously. 'Help you,' I tried. I did a few more signs which I hoped meant doctor or nurse. These weren't the usual terms we practiced. In the end, he gave me a strange look, almost seemed to laugh, and then he let the paramedics stretcher him away. We all stood somewhat breathlessly in the store, hands and hearts aflutter, trying to calm down after the scare.

To my surprise, one of the paramedics returned to the store a few days later. 'I just wanted to thank you for helping us out,' he said. 'We had a translator at the hospital. You may just have saved his life.'

'That's awesome,' I muttered happily, not sure what else to say.

'He was apparently given the wrong medication once, in a similar situation, because no one would listen to him. So that's why he was fighting. The patient wanted to thank you as well.' The paramedic turned to leave. 'But he did have a question for you.'

'What was that?' I asked.

'He wanted to know why you kept calling him a blue chicken?'

I was sure I was saying doctor, but no one needed to know. 'Different language,' I lied, 'ASL. Must have been lost in translation.'

The paramedic nodded but didn't look convinced. He had a funny smile on his face. 'Well, thanks anyway. You saved a blue chicken this week, and that's no small thing.'

Ten

CLEAN UP IN AISLE FOUR

I began working at the local grocery store quite by accident. I put in countless unpaid hours in my dad's hardware store, but I was keen to have some pocket money. So I came up with a scheme where I waited around the parking lot of the local grocery store for older customers struggling with their bags. The store had a metal guard rail to prevent customers from taking the carts into the parking lot, so it meant many elderly people struggled to transfer their bags to their vehicles. That's where I came in. 'May I help you to your car?' I would ask pleasantly, as though I just happened to be walking by. The person said yes almost every time, and most of them offered me a tip afterwards. I became quite expert at saying no, explaining that I couldn't possibly accept money for being a good Samaritan, and discovered that it often had the effect of doubling the tip. For the first two weekends I did this, I earned a pretty penny.

On the third weekend I arrived to discover that half a dozen kids had taken up positions strategically around the doors. Word of my innovative small business had got around and everyone was trying to horn in. Unfortunately, most of these fly-by-nights did not have the grace and sophistication that I brought to the table. Indeed, because so many kids had shown up, they were all jostling aggressively to get to the customers. The older folks felt quite intimidated, and in a few instances, kids had forcibly grabbed the grocery bag and a tug of war had ensued. At least once the produce had exploded from the paper bag and scattered around the lot.

It didn't take long for Fresh Foods to hire their own staff to assist customers. They removed the guard rails and increased the number of assistants who escorted clients to their cars. In less than a month my brilliant small business had been replaced by a corporate giant and was no more. One of the managers, though, had noticed me, and quite by chance he offered me a job inside the store, even though I was years younger than all the other employees. That was how I became a stacker, loading and unloading the pallets, and then stocking the shelves throughout the day as needed. It was a perfect job because I had complete flexibility, and as long as I was available at peak times, the manager didn't really care what I did.

I was often assigned to the check-out counters. My job was to unpack cans of soup on the counter where customers waited to pay, and then when it was busy, I helped to package the groceries. It was a cumbersome job. I had the crates hidden behind the counter, tripping up the check-out lady, all because management didn't want people to see the messy boxes. I also had to unpack the blue, zippered canvas bags that were Fresh Foods' trademark and which they gave away with larger orders. Then I had to ignore all of that and either run around the counter to stack, in the hopes that people would be enticed by whatever we had on display that day or run to the end of the conveyor belt and package up the groceries as they were slowly priced and processed.

One afternoon as we were doing this a masked intruder thrust a knife at us. I was working beside arguably the most ferociously cranky woman I've ever encountered, Mrs. Antoine. Her stare alone could cause tough street hoodlums to defecate in fear. If I was to be trapped with a criminal, she would be the person I'd want at my side to mop the floor with the assailant. Or so I thought. To my dismay, she crumbled like jelly when he pulled the knife. I was too bemused by the guy's balaclava to actually be scared. He had a stupid blue wool hat that he'd hastily pulled down to cover his face, and the eye-holes were poorly aligned. He looked, frankly, like a demented sock puppet. But the knife was real, and Mrs. Antoine's squeal, though muted, was blood curdling. So high that I was sure only dogs and kids could hear it.

'Give me one of those bags,' he whisper-screamed at me, trying not to attract attention, and then to Mrs. Antoine, 'Empty the cash.' Her hands were shaking so much that she couldn't do it. 'You!' he said to me. 'Do it!' I squeezed in front of her and put all the bills into the bag. Mrs. Antoine was not a small woman, so it wasn't easy fitting in front of her. As I pulled away, I dropped the bag. I scrambled to pick it up, zipped the bag, and then the guy ripped it out of my hands, cutting me in the process, and ran from the store.

The manager saw the commotion and rushed over to us. Mrs. Antoine was blubbering like a baby. 'He had a knife!' she shouted. 'Took the bag with all the money. He was going to stab me.' On and on she went.

The manager looked at me with concern. My body was shaking, and I realized suddenly that I was more terrified than I'd realized. Adrenaline had kept me going. 'You okay?' he asked. I could tell he was trying to appear caring, but his eyes kept flicking towards the open cash register. 'How much did he take?' he finally gushed unable to feign empathy any longer.

Mrs. Antoine still couldn't speak. 'Don't worry,' I answered for her. 'He didn't get anything.' I reached down and put the blue canvas bag on the conveyor belt. It was full of cash.

The manager looked confused. 'What was in the other bag?' he asked.

'I threw in a couple of soup cans and zipped it up. I switched them when I dropped the bag.'

As I said this the Assistant-Manager's voice came over the loudspeaker: 'Clean up in Aisle Four,' he called, and I started to move in that direction.

The manager stopped me with his hand. 'Not you!' he said with a huge grin on his face. 'Consider this a paid vacation.'

'Wow!' I said. 'Never had one of those. Thank you. How long have I got?'

He looked at me, confused. 'Today,' he answered matter-of-factly. 'Be back for your shift tomorrow.'

Well okay, I thought, two hours left on my shift. Better than nothing, I suppose. But the entire way home I kept checking over my shoulder in case the bad guy came after me brandishing a can of tomato soup.

PART TWO

In which our hero leaves the comfort of the known world behind

Eleven

APOCALYPSE, NOW

It was the best of times, it was the worst of times. It was a time of hope and yet the light at the end of the tunnel was actually an on-coming train. As graduation approached we all prepared to leave our beloved elementary school behind. St. Hopeless of the Unwanted (not its real name), was not only casting us off into the wilderness, but it was also shutting its doors for good. It's probably true to say that this was a tender mercy. The building would have been precarious when it was new, but in its doddery old age it was downright dangerous. Neighbourhood redistribution also meant that there just weren't as many kids and the opening of a brand-new English school nearby had sucked the funding and interest out of the community.

Of course, just because we complained all the time and denigrated the teachers whenever we had the chance, did not mean we had anything better in mind. And for the sophisticated ones among us who had outgrown the institution and were ready for the next phase in the thrilling adventure we called underfunded public education, the prospect of moving to a new establishment was daunting. At least the nearby French high school was reputed to have brand new classrooms and modern facilities. It was easier to get to from my place than even my elementary school, and of course I would at least have all my pals to accompany me on this savage rite of passage. This, in truth, was the greatest godsend of all: that I didn't have to make the journey alone.

One afternoon we all gathered in the pock-marked school yard and reminisced about our lost youth. J.P. was fondly recounting the drole story of how he had been wedged in the basketball hoop by the older kids when he was in first grade. He left out the part about wetting his pants while he waited for the teachers to come and rescue him, but the story was moving and touching all the same.

I debated what poignant moment I should lead with. In my first year of school my disconcertingly buxom teacher insisted on tying my left hand behind my back to force me to use my right hand. Every morning the principal would burst into the classroom and untie me, chastising the teacher for adhering to a now banned practice. 'Pretend the left-handers are normal,' he announced one time. I felt special.

I told the witty and provocative story about the removal of my rights and freedoms, though admittedly I focused mostly on the prominence of her bosoms. Even all these many years later I remember the feel of her breasts on my little face and the smell of her perfume. Once, in a more intimate setting, my best friend had informed me that her bosoms were a D cup, and I remember thinking how unkind that such magnificent appurtenances should be given virtually a failing grade. Oh, how bitter it was to kiss those precious moments of childhood goodbye.

I had not appreciated until that moment how difficult it would have been for Neil Armstrong to leave the moon, for 50 million immigrants to leave their homes during the war and travel to a new world, or for my uncle Thierry to have his penis removed after the unfortunate encounter with the woodchipper. Now I understood. Like them, I would be leaving it all behind never to be seen again. Well except for my uncle who kept it in a glass jar, but that's another story.

Replete with nostalgia, I headed home prepared for a relaxing summer away from the high stress of the classroom, ready to prepare myself for the next action-packed chapter of my life. Cue the light at the end of the tunnel; reveal that it's a train. I knew as soon as I got in the apartment that something was amiss. It is never comforting when your mother greets you with, 'Now I don't want you to worry,' especially if your father, who is rarely at home in the early afternoon, is sitting uncomfortably at the kitchen table. We had not had many of these in my life, but in later years I would come to call these an intervention.

'Son, we've made a decision,' she said in English. I wish I could recall the way the conversation unfolded, but in truth, as soon as she started speaking, I stopped listening. I felt my world collapse. My head started throbbing and I felt such a palpitation in my chest that I thought my heart was trying to break free. I remember scrambling to sit down, head bowed, shaking. 'No, no, no,' I whispered, 'you can't do this.'

My mother came to my side and tried to grab my hand, but I had my fists bunched so tightly that she couldn't prise my fingers free. 'It's for the best,' she said, but I could hear the desperation in her voice. 'Say something,' she added, but she wasn't speaking to me.

My father moved his chair closer to mine. 'Hey,' he said in French. 'Écoute. Have I ever asked you to do something that I didn't think was right? Ever?' I shook my head. 'That's right. Because I never would. But this can change your life. Give you all the advantages I never had. It's the way the world works, and I don't want you to have the same limitations I had. Understand?' I refused to answer. He waited beside me for a few more minutes and then put his hand on my shoulder. 'It's for the best.' Then he rose and headed back to the store. My mother, despairing, ran to the fridge and started to make a chocolate sundae for me. 'Your favourite.'

When I finally got away, I headed straight for the train tracks where my gang always gathered. All four were there, laughing and kidding around, the freedom of summer already upon them. But they saw me coming and they saw my face.

'Holy crap!' J.P. shouted. 'What happened? It's gotta be bad.'

I threw myself down in the gravel beside the track and buried my face in my hands. 'It's not fair,' I screamed, and everyone gathered around. That was the gift of friendship, of familiarity. A shoulder to lean on instantly.

'What happened?' Laurence said, and the tone of her voice just sent the tears flowing.

'They're sending me to English school!' I cried.

'But what about us?' J.P. screamed. 'We're a gang. A team. We can't speak English.'

'I know,' I said miserably. 'I'll have to go alone.'

Everyone sat down, all in a line. We felt the rumbling beneath us and waited as the train sped towards us. The wind and chaos of a passing train, especially sitting only two feet away, seemed to be a metaphor for everything we were feeling. When the silence settled again someone asked: 'Where?'

'Up the road, right?' J.P. answered for me. 'That thing's a monster.'

The light was fading from the late evening sky and the air was getting chilly. Without saying a word, we all rose in unison and headed home. Our apartments were lined up one next to the other. As we reached our respective homes everyone peeled away without speaking: J.P. and his brother first, Laurence and her brother next, and then me. Alone. I guess it was time for me to get used to it.

Twelve

INFERNO

If the transition to junior high was difficult for most, my parents decided to make the challenge exponentially greater. My father, not hitherto known for barbaric savagery, suddenly developed a psychopathic craving to do ill and decided to send me to an English school so that I could perfect the language. And there was more. In elementary school I had been placed in an experimental advanced class, one that progressed twice as quickly through all the regular lessons, meaning that I — and a select group of lab rats, six in all — was almost two years ahead of my classmates. By the time I'd reached the end of my elementary school I was in fact two years younger than the average graduating student. Two years younger, and two years shorter.

To make matters worse, the only school that would accept an accelerated student was Grand Inquisitor Comprehensive High School, the largest, meanest and poorest school in the English system. Had it been a year sooner the school would not have been able to accept me. It was a girl's school only. But the year I graduated was the year it became a comprehensive institution, doubling in size overnight as it accepted its first intake of boys. Although I didn't know it at the time, 90% of the original teachers, all nuns, would be driven from the school by this feral pack of Y chromosomes within the first month. And while I have no evidence of this, it is possibly because student admissions were based on candidates successfully demonstrating unmitigated psychopathic tendencies.

It will already be difficult for the reader to imagine a more desperately perverted scenario in which a child might be sent to his death, and yet somehow, the worst was yet to come. My mother, forever in denial about our poverty and position in life, insisted on presenting me to the world as what she imagined might be an aristocrat. Alas, her sense of style was influenced by a truly personal and idiosyncratic understanding of posh clothing and behaviour, coupled with our financial inability to afford the luxury to which she aspired. So, she improvised.

I'm not sure if I have set the scene sufficiently well for my first day of school, but imagine a child two feet shorter than the average student, dressed in plaid corduroy trousers that were too short even for his diminutive frame, speaking with a thick French accent, set adrift among territorial cannibals who hated foreigners, in an environment where the would-be game-wardens were having nervous breakdowns and hiding in the teachers' lounge refusing to confront the masses. If the phrase human piñata to describe me comes to mind, then you are not far off.

My 'new' school was in the midst of a funding crisis, an identity crisis, and a building crisis. Its aging infrastructure had barely survived when a 1000 girls traversed the narrow hallways; but it lasted mere days under the onslaught of an additional 1200 Neanderthals

— boys, moreover, who were ripped from surrounding schools against their will, in an experiment that tried to marry different linguistic and cultural communities, coupled with a variety of educationally challenged groups for whom a change of scene was thought to be the remedy to staggering failure rates, truancy and gang violence. For those who have read Dante: my new school was literally the ninth circle of hell. And I was the crash-test dummy that was sent in to test its limits.

I feel I have already set a staggeringly unbelievable scenario without adding my own personal idiosyncrasies into the equation. It will chill your blood to hear that I believed arriving armed with intimidating works of literature and a razor-sharp wit would protect me from the heathens, the way a crucifix and a garlic necklace might ward off vampires. And so, on day one I brought a copy of James Joyce's *Finnegans Wake* with me, an impossibly difficult novel at the best of times, but simply incomprehensible for a child, including, let's be honest, me. But I had set myself the challenge that summer of reading through it, with the hope of understanding its contents at a later date. I was equally sure that should a misunderstanding occur in the hallways of hell, I could casually make reference to the book and then distract menacing trolls and ogres with a chirpy discourse on contemporary Irish writing. What could go wrong?

Did I mention the thick Coke-bottle glasses I had just been given and an ill-fitting set of braces? Even if I could pull off the complex 'th' sound of the English language, the metal contraption in my mouth made me sound like a robot from a badly dubbed science fiction film. So, there you have it. I was ready to conquer the world.

My mother hugged me tightly. Unfortunately, she did this in full view of the ridiculously cool and ferociously intimidating kids arriving in their droves. 'You look fabulous,' she said, with the full weight and myopia of a mother's love. 'And remember. You're smarter than everyone here. You'll be king of the castle in no time.' She kissed me again and then launched me into the wilds, the way salmon might be released beneath raging rapids guarded by famished grizzly bears. I studied the intimidating architecture of the building: barred windows, broken brickwork that someone later called prison chic, and a graffiti-lined entranceway.

When I got to the door, ready to conquer my new kingdom, a tall, mean-faced kid, who I later learned was Ronald Turgeon, stopped me in my tracks. 'What are you supposed to be, Mama's boy?' he sneered. A pack of his sycophants encircled me like hyenas.

'Have you read James Joyce?' I asked pleasantly, holding *Finnegans* up for his delectation. Before I knew it, the book was smashing down on my head and I found myself in a garbage bin beside the door. It took me a moment to extract myself, and a few more to find my glasses in a nearby shrub. By the time I got in I was late for roll call, whatever that was. A crusty-faced man, who I later discovered was the Vice-Principal, pointed at me as I walked into the gym. 'You. Late. Principal's office.' I stood for a moment, blinking, and then followed the direction of his gnarled finger. Another teacher, at the entrance to the gym, handed me a piece of paper and pointed down another corridor. I made my way there and as I walked, I realized I didn't have my good luck novel. If my day was disastrous with my lucky talisman, I could only imagine the desolation that awaited without it.

When I arrived at the reception area, I handed my note to a stern looking lady. After an interminable wait, I was directed to the principal's office. He looked at the note and said: 'Hold out your hands.' I wasn't sure why, but I was nervous that they might be dirty from my earlier skirmish. I need not have worried. Without warning he pulled out a thick leather strap and smacked my hands with all his might with five savage blows. I looked at my hands, still floating in front of me, and watched as the skin went from preternaturally white to purply red. I felt the water rise in my eyes. 'I didn't do anything,' I started to say, and the principal brandished the strap.

'Do you want another set?' He pointed at his door, dismissing me, and turned away before an answer came to mind.

I made my way back along the corridor to the gym, which was now empty, and wondered what I was meant to do. I was standing there, lost, looking at my hands when a teacher found me. She saw my hands, folded open towards the ceiling the way I prayed at mass, and then at my puffy eyes. 'Oh, you poor little soul. Bloody barbarians. Come on. Let's get you settled.' She was a young nun but dressed in modern clothes. She introduced herself as Sister Anne. 'First days are the worst. Right?' I blinked up at her but didn't respond. 'The first 300 days are the worst, right?' she repeated jokingly. A tear ran down my cheek. She wiped it away with her thumb. 'It'll get better. Okay? I promise.' I nodded, more grateful than she could know.

She took my hand and led me to my first class. She introduced me to my homeroom teacher and waited until I'd found my seat. When I looked up my guardian angel smiled, nodded, and left the room. I glanced at the clock and my heart sank. Only an hour of junior high had passed. 299 days and 6 hours still to go. But who was counting?

Thirteen

GUARDIAN ANGEL

Virtually everyone has a horror story to tell about school. It's why Hollywood is obsessed with this period and reworks the drama of youth so often. Even as a young person I knew this, and so I kept the tragedy of my day a secret. I had gone past the grades my parents had reached, and I knew that for them every step I took along the path was a victory against their difficult past. Who was I to ruin their dream? When I returned grimly to the over-heated apartment, my mother baking up a celebratory storm to mark my triumphant first day of junior high, I didn't have the heart to tell them how utterly I had failed.

'The school's so big!' my mother gushed, 'I'm so proud of you for knowing your way around. Change isn't easy.'

'We trained him well,' my father joked, the guilt of sending me to English school still weighing heavily on him. 'They can't throw anything at him that he can't handle.' He patted me on the back, brusquely and playfully, but his hand lingered a moment. For him, this was downright demonstrative.

'Oh, for goodness' sake!' my mother cried, 'Get over here,' and she proceeded to squeeze me with such force I was relatively certain my internal organs were oozing from my ears. I smiled and made up a story about all the people I'd met. I described the school in extraordinary detail even though, once I'd entered its halls, all I really studied was the worn linoleum. Eye contact, I quickly intuited, was potentially lethal. There was one moment when the strategy paid off. Rounding a corner, I ran into a young girl wearing a low-cut top and smacked my face into her prominent bosom. This did not happen at Elementary school. She slammed me back against the locker without sparing me a second glance. The feeling of her skin on my lips, though, carried me through the rest of that wretched afternoon.

At one point, as I was heading to another class, I saw Ronald Turgeon and his posse holding court. I had a decision to make. I could brave the congo line of punches or wait until they'd gone and accept the late slip. Detention, after all, wasn't the worst thing that could happen, though I didn't think I could handle the strap again. As I stood there, however, a tall, lean figure entered the frame. 'I don't suppose you're heading this way?' Sister Anne asked, a glint in her eye. 'I hate going anywhere on my own. Mind if I join you?'

I am not proud to admit that I actually giggled. Just a little. 'Okay,' I said. 'If it helps you out.'

It was Sister Anne's turn to giggle. 'I like you. I think we're going to be good friends.' With that we sailed down the turbulent waters of the Amazon River entirely unmolested by the crocodiles.

When I got to my classroom, I shook her hand awkwardly. 'Thanks, Miss. That guy's got it in for me.'

'Yeah, well I'll spread the word that you're under my protection.' She said it with a fake Italian accent, like a Mafia boss, but then she caught the concern on my face. 'Don't worry. I'll do it discreetly. We wouldn't want anyone to accuse you of being a teacher's pet. But there are ways.' Dagnammit if I didn't giggle again. Just slightly. In a manly way. She smiled. 'You and me buddy. We're a team.'

'No, nothing special happened,' I assured my parents. 'Just the usual. First day stuff. Giving us the list of books, the lunch schedule, clubs. Same old, same old.'

My father smiled. 'Such a man of the world,' he said, and ruffled my hair. 'Okay, I have to go back to the store,' he added.

'But dinner,' my mother protested. 'It's almost ready.'

He grabbed her by the waist and dipped her, like a ballroom dancer. 'And I'll be back. Who can resist food prepared by a goddess?'

My mother smacked him playfully on the arm. 'Go then, you big French brute.' But she was smiling and blushing deeply.

'I'm going to wash up,' I told her. 'Let me know if you need help to set the table.'

'Not tonight,' she said. 'Tonight, you're the guest of honour.'

I made my way into the tiny bathroom and pulled up my shirt. The bruises the boys had given me were blooming like funereal flowers. Black chrysanthemums. 'Tomorrow,' I thought, 'tomorrow is another day.' But I still collapsed in a ball in the corner of the shower, letting the hot water burn my skin.

To my surprise, the following day was better. The aggression was there, but Turgeon and his gang held back, scowling menacingly, but keeping their distance. I kept my head down. I didn't fully understand what was happening, but I wasn't complaining. I made my way to Homeroom, then my next class, still nothing. At lunch I was sitting alone in one corner of the cafeteria, having scoped out at least one exit route, when a shadow loomed over me. I looked up nervously but was relieved to see Sister Anne. She had her hands on her hips, as though she was angry with me, but her voice was complicit: 'So? How's it going so far?'

I looked around furtively and then positively gushed: 'What did you do? He didn't come anywhere near me. His guys left me alone.'

Sister Anne was nodding. 'Nice. I let it be known that you were my cousin and that you were my responsibility.'

'You lied!' I said, completely shocked. My faith, I have to admit, was crumbling right before my eyes. 'But you're a nun!'

She leaned in close and whispered, 'That's why God invented Confession.' She punched me softly on the arm. Then her face got serious. I had seen the gentle side of this lady but not the steel. 'I also told the principal that if he ever used the strap on another student, I'd report him to the school board. Bloody savage.'

I was fighting off tears. 'You're not allowed to marry me, are you?' I said, giggling just a little.

'Let me check with Fr. Rémi. I believe the rules are a bit fuzzy on that one.'

Fourteen

OUT OF AFRICA

I don't want to suggest that life in junior high became instantly bearable just because I had a powerful ally, but what I realized was that having a sense of hope made all the difference. It was still a tough school, the nuns were leaving in droves, and the bullies were having a field day, but somehow knowing I had Sister Anne in my court made everything tolerable. School ecosystems are complex, and the wildlife quickly finds its place on the food chain. The apex predators claim their territory instantly, the parasites quickly attach themselves to whatever organism can offer protection and sustenance, and loners chart their spot, usually perched in high altitudes just slightly out of reach. The rest of the lesser life forms navigate the Serengeti based on instinct and luck.

What also became clear was that the climate made a big difference to our comfort. If the winds blew fair and the grasses grew in abundance, if the waterholes were full to overflowing, there was usually room for all of us to co-exist. When the weather turned, however, and drought set in, the animals circled each other more intently, ready to steal one another's food source, or head in for the

kill. In those early weeks of school the plains of Africa were plentiful: the rules were somewhat relaxed as everybody found their
groove; the equipment in the gyms and cafeteria hadn't yet broken
so everyone had access to what they needed; and the teachers were
leaving at breakneck speed so that made the workload bearable in
the classroom. At such times the predators were content merely
with petty violence: roughing you up at the locker, stealing a lunch
here and there, an occasional but usually half-hearted beating in
the schoolyard. Life was good.

This moment of calm allowed the minor critters to find their
rightful place in the food chain. I had looked up the taxonomy of
animals in the hopes that there was a cool classification below apex
predators that I could inhabit. Unfortunately, the only other cate-
gory I found was 'prey', which I refused to believe about myself. I
was wise enough, however, to understand that just because I didn't
consider myself a steak dinner didn't mean the carnivores agreed.
So, I studied the landscape carefully to understand the ebb and
flow. I saw how the vulnerable survived — or not — and then pur-
sued option one.

It was in the course of doing this life-saving research that I
made one of my most important discoveries. One bully who mate-
rialized in my Art class, a kid called Sheriff of all things, developed
a natural antipathy for me. He made a point in every class of trying
to pick a fight when the teacher wasn't looking or knocking all my
things off my desk as he passed by. It was usually resolved by a
quick shoving match in class, and even though he was slightly taller
than me, I found that I could hold my own with him. At first. Early
skirmishes saw us evenly matched. As term went on, though, I no-

ticed he was becoming increasingly agile, and definitely stronger. I had to investigate. What I discovered changed my life. Sheriff, it turns out, had joined the gymnastics team, and he was rapidly gaining flexibility and strength. After one tussle he actually pushed me across the classroom and I landed so forcefully against a stack of chairs that I had trouble walking for the rest of the day.

Although I tried never to reveal any of these issues to my parents, my father was quick to notice. He pinned me down in the store after hours. This is where we always had our most meaningful conversations, usually choreographed around an activity of some sort: weighing the nails, organizing the shelves, unpacking the paint crates. On this night he could plainly see that I was limping, and he used his master interrogation skills to wrench the truth out of me. 'What happened?' he asked, and all the weeks of pent-up frustration came gushing out. I ended with one last exclamation that, mercifully, he didn't question too carefully: 'And Sister Anne said she can't marry me after all!'

With that he hugged me and then we returned to our task at hand. That night we were transferring the contents of huge bundles of peat moss into smaller packages which our customers preferred for their indoor plants. The smell was intoxicating; soothing. As was always the case my father began mid-sentence. 'So Jean-Louis, the class bully, always had it in for me. I don't know why. I was the youngest of 13 children, so I knew how to be invisible, but this guy just had my number. He'd follow me everywhere. He'd steal my lunch. He'd punch me out. But my dad, your grandfather, was a real angry guy, scary violent. I vowed I would never be the same.'

I'd never heard my father speak so much all in one go. He looked a bit exhausted, as though he couldn't quite believe it himself. I didn't want to say a thing in case I broke the spell. 'But I had a secret weapon. Every day after school I had to help my father unload cement trucks. As a result, my arms, even for a small guy, were like iron. My dad said, if a guy ever bugs you, just grab him and hold on until he gets bored. It didn't seem very efficient, but it actually worked. With everybody except Jean-Louis. One day at school he came at me, threw my lunch on the ground and stepped on it. I lost my temper and pushed him into the fence. His head went between the metal bars and he got stuck there. It took an hour for the school to get him loose. Had to cut one of the bars with a metal saw.' My father chuckled. 'He never picked on me again.'

'Did you get in trouble?'

'They wanted to give me a month's detention after school, but my father explained that two hours of unloading 80-pound concrete bags every night was worse than anything they could do to me. The Jesuit priests who taught us loved the idea of manual labour, and that was that.'

'So what are you recommending exactly?' I asked.

'Join the gymnastics club too.' And that was how I became a gymnast.

What I didn't realize until I was vetted and accepted by the coach, Mr. Deiter, was that many of the school bullies were on the team. An unwritten code seemed to be that the bullies didn't pick on guys in their 'gang', even the amoebas like me. In one fell swoop, it seemed, I had removed fifty percent of the predators from the Serengeti plains; another sizeable portion stayed clear because they didn't want to antagonize the toughest kids on the team indirectly. Sister Anne had nullified my mortal enemy and his group of hyenas. All I had to look out for were the occasional poachers who didn't follow any rules of the natural order. Life, it seemed, instantly became more promising. Sheriff was still an idiot, but he was clearly confused by my new status. We fought, but some of the sheer joy of the fight was lost for him. Who knew a guy with an IQ of three could feel morally conflicted? Perhaps I was being a tad unkind. I was sure his IQ was in the double digits.

What was also true is that my social life opened up in other ways, almost immediately. I met the person who would become my best school pal, Karl Gunter, and I also began to appreciate that the world was filled with women who weren't nuns or teachers. I'm not sure if I'd ever studied a leotard with much attention before, but I certainly couldn't unsee it once it hit my senses. To my utter amazement, the boys in the gymnastics club were expected — nay, mandated — to assist the girls with their floor routines, so that once I actually placed my hand on a young lady's back. On purpose and without getting in trouble. The only thing that had ever made my heart beat that quickly prior to this was when Turgeon and his cronies had beaten me to a pulp earlier in the year. This was decidedly more pleasant.

The joys of this new world order, however, didn't fully make sense until one evening after school. I was leaving late after a compulsory workout, and I unfortunately stumbled onto one of the Italian gangs that hated the gym jocks. I was flattered, mind you, that they characterized my scrawny self in that way, but the result was that three of the guys pummeled me and threw me into one of the bushes near the school entrance. They turned towards me to finish the work they'd started, but as I prepared for a heroic death, I saw my gym jocks rush from the building. In no time the giants from our club had dispersed the thugs that had waylaid me.

Sheriff, of all people, was one of my rescuers. He looked towards me in the hedge. 'You okay, shithead?'

'Yup,' I said. 'I had them just where I wanted.' He looked like he had just changed his mind about helping me and wanted to finish the job the Italian kids had started. 'I'm okay — thanks to Sheriff and his deputies.'

He paused for a minute and then seemed to like the sound of that. 'Whatever,' he said, but he had a smile on his face as he walked away.

And with that my chalk-covered, muscle-bound posse left me to my own devices. I sat there for a moment, catching my breath. I have to be honest. I was somewhat elated. No one had ever stood up for me before, even if it was a half-hearted, mechanical act. I dusted myself off and then, as I was about to leave, I saw a mangled book sitting in the dirt. I picked it up. It was my copy of *Finnegans Wake*. 'There you are old friend,' I said, and James Joyce and I headed out of Africa for home.

Fifteen

HALLELUJAH

It is easy, with the benefit of hindsight, to criticize those of limited vision who failed to appreciate genius when they encountered it. The record producer who quashed the release of Leonard Cohen's 'Hallelujah', for example, or the executive who told Queen that 'Bohemian Rhapsody' was a structural mess, and he wouldn't represent them.

So it was for me and our bi-monthly Science Fair. I had always participated, and though I always did best when I conformed to convention — a *papier mâché* volcano filled with bicarbonate of soda that erupted with a sprinkling of vinegar which got sixth prize — I always felt that the school was narrow in their definition of innovation. When I was working truly outside the box, they simply didn't get it. I'm convinced that this narrow-minded rejection has influenced me to this day, compelling me to be more daring, more charismatic and more debonair.

At the time, though, it weighed me down. I did a fair bit to support the local church, even though Fr. Rémi usually begged me not to, so I understood the difficult lot of the saints and martyrs who struggled when their goodness was persecuted and shut down. I certainly didn't put myself in their league, but I tempered my disappointment by reassuring myself with feel-good Catholic narratives of people who were cooked alive for their faith, who lost their eyes or were disemboweled. How could I complain that my Science Fair project was rejected when I still had my spleen? Cold comfort, but comfort nonetheless.

And so when Mr. Franklyn announced the parameters for the year's Science Fair, I did not exactly jump for joy. The initial tinge of excitement was quickly quashed. 'Don't build your hopes up!' I said to myself sternly.

Maria Vianetti, the science nerd and class darling looked over at me. 'You planning to be rejected again this time?' she said, venom dripping from her future Nobel-Prize-for-Science lips.

'Actually,' I answered before my brain was even consulted, 'I have a project that is going to blow the roof off this place.'

She snorted. 'Your last improvised bomb was banned before it could be displayed,' she cackled.

'This time I was speaking metaphorically,' I said, sweat beginning to pool in my armpits. 'You've heard of a metaphor, right? A figure of speech that compares something using like or as.'

'That's a simile, Nimrod,' she answered disdainfully. I was about to follow up with more brilliant repartee, but Mr. Franklyn called her to the front of the class to explain a particularly difficult equation that he was struggling with. 'I'd be happy to help,' she said sweetly, but her eyes were drilling savagely into mine.

After class my friend Karl pushed me into the lockers. 'What the hell were you thinking?' he said. 'No one takes on Vianetti. They give her the first prize ahead of time.'

'I know,' I whined miserably. 'She just always gets under my skin. She's like an elephant. She never forgets even your smallest mistakes.'

'Okay to be fair, the explosives you rigged in first term blew up the large garbage bin after the Fair. That was pretty memorable.'

I was nodding. I felt better. 'Yeah,' I agreed, 'It was pretty cool. Totally worth the suspension.'

Karl patted me on the shoulder. 'Atta boy. Now what are you going to do for an encore? You've pretty much challenged the science queen to a duel.'

'I actually have an idea. An invention I've been thinking about for decades. It will revolutionize health care.'

Karl was nodding. 'Okay buddy. I have faith in you.'

I was totally surprised. 'You do?'

'No dufous. You suck at science. But prove me wrong.'

The lead up to the Science Fair was always exciting. The nerds actually got to claim one of the gyms for the first time, displacing all the jocks for two solid weeks. Their frustration was palpable and ridiculously funny. I was in the gym club so it affected me directly. We had to ration out the remaining gym time in a mathematically complicated process where basketball handed over to volleyball which surrendered to gymnastics and then dodge ball, all rotating around the mandated physical fitness classes we had to take as part of our curriculum. It was chaos. But for someone like me who wasn't a true jock, and who participated mostly to keep the bullies at bay, it was funny to hear the locker room chatter and the deep existential angst the situation generated. I always commiserated with the jocks when they looked my way, but I was secretly relieved. To be a member of the gym club meant you had to attend seven am compulsory rotations, lunchtime practice and then evening training a minimum three times a week. The Fair provided a reprieve of sorts and gave me my mornings back.

I decided to use the extra time to develop my Science Fair contribution, and I felt that, in order to be successful, I had to make more of an effort to get into the science teacher's good books. Mr. Franklyn was by far the most popular science teacher in the entire school but he was a couple of test tubes short of a science kit. We had been waiting for years for the school to provide us with a pressurized glass cannister and the day it arrived he unveiled it with excitement. 'This contraption proves that air pressure is stronger than concrete,' he announced proudly. He then invited each of us to approach and try to compress the lever. The perfect seal, of course, meant that the air essentially became a concrete block. No one could move it.

As the experiment proceeded, however, Mr. Franklyn seemed to get frustrated that the device was performing as it was meant to, and when the last student had had a chance to try, he placed the cylinder on the floor. No one knew what he was planning until it was too late. He took a step back and then jumped on the handle of the contraption which, being mostly glass, promptly shattered into a thousand pieces. We could hear the tinkling of the glass shards in the deathly silence that followed. The cylinder had cost the entire science budget for the year. 'Well,' he finally announced, 'I guess it was faulty.' Everyone looked down at their notes while he went out to fetch a broom.

'That's going to be you,' Maria whispered, as she made a great show of spreading out the plans to her Science Fair contribution. It honestly looked like the detailed modeling of a nuclear reactor. 'Or have you decided to put yourself out of our misery and skip the Science Fair?'

'You can laugh now,' I responded, affecting a sly grin that seemed to rattle her confidence, 'but this time I have something that will blow ... amaze everyone. It will go straight to market for development.' That detail definitely fazed her. She started to say something, but then looked down at her plans somewhat more critically. Had she misjudged? Did I have an ace up my sleeve? Was this month going to be her last as queen of the fair? These were all questions that I was sure she was asking herself.

'Good luck with your delusions,' she announced and left the room, but without her usual bravado.

I made my way to the front of the class and grabbed the broom from Mr. Franklyn. 'Let me help,' I said, and he seemed grateful for the company.

'I think the principal will be pissed,' he said, and then remembering who he was speaking to corrected himself. 'A tad annoyed.' He seemed genuinely upset with himself. 'I don't know why I thought the cannister would respond differently this time.'

'You jumped on it once before?'

'Of course. That's how we broke the last one.'

'We?'

'There's got to be a way to get that stupid lever to compress.'

'But isn't the whole point of it that it doesn't? It has one purpose.'

Mr. Franklyn paused then. 'You know, if you set your limits based on people's expectations, you will always be disappointed.'

I nodded enthusiastically. 'Exactly. That's why I wanted to speak with you about my idea for the Science Fair. I think this idea is a winner.'

'Does it explode?' he asked apprehensively.

'Not even a whiff of smoke this time. I've learned my lesson, and I take to heart what you just said. Think outside the box. That's what I'm planning. It's a sure thing.'

Mr. Franklyn was visibly relieved. 'Well okay then! It'll be tough to dethrone the queen, but even a strong second or third place showing … even fourth or fifth … you know, sixth or a participation badge … anyway, whatever, you know, I'm proud of you for thinking you have a chance.' And with those sterling words of encouragement he left the room leaving me to clean up the debris. Lesson learned: I was on my own. Then again, given his demonstrated IQ I was probably safer that way. I headed home and straight to my father's small workshop.

Despite all the affected cynicism that my age group typically displayed, the day of the Science Fair was actually a big deal. There was incredible energy in the building, and my parents had even floated the possibility that they might attend. I knew it wasn't going to happen. My father worked sixteen hours a day and had never shut the store, and my mother was too nervous to attend school events without him. But usually they just assured me they couldn't make it, so even the fictional note of intent had meant a lot to me.

I signed in on the day and was given my table. To my relief I was on another side of the gym from Maria Vianetti. Admittedly only because the school tended to organize the booths in order of likely award winners, so Maria was always right up against the podium. The distance from my broken table, however, was a relief. Not only did Maria have the newly laminated display table to work from, but her father, a printer, had also prepared extraordinary signage for her booth. Mine, in comparison, looked like a reject from an Oliver Twist orphanage: the table was cracked and lopsided, my poster board had been rained on so the red ink from the marker had bled everywhere. My poster, from a distance, looked like an advertisement for a blood clinic after it had been ransacked by Dracula. But no matter. My project, which sat hidden under a brown cardboard box, was ready to be unveiled, when, and only when, the judges arrived.

No one else had used this strategy before so there was a bit of buzz. There was also a fair bit of controversy. Two of the participants, twins as it turned out, had made a point to create 'statements', as they put it, essentially a protest at the 'commodification of student knowledge.' In their view, pitting students against each other was unhelpful, capitalistic, and 'soul destroying.' Their booths were therefore half protest, half parody. Halley Bollo was the intellectual of the two. Her booth proudly announced: 'We, Robot. How schools are instruments of the fascist state — turning our children into mindless automatons.' Marcus Bollo had taken a different approach: he went for shock value. 'Our most Underappreciated Muscle: Give your Sphincter some love.' I won't describe the images he'd chosen to illustrate his message. Suffice to say that the school administrators were busy trying to tear down the offensive materials before too many parents, and especially the school trustees saw them, and the twins' parents, notorious protest-era hippies were claiming that their kids' first amendment rights were being violated. I wanted to tell them that we were in Canada so it didn't apply, but that would have meant leaving my booth unattended.

Unfortunately, with all the commotion, Maria found an opportunity to make her way over to me and she poked contemptuously at my box. 'Too ashamed to let anyone see it, huh?'

I moved protectively to keep the box in place. 'I wish you every success, Maria. Congratulations on winning first prize.' That threw her completely. I wasn't known for my magnanimity, and usually I let my tone of voice make my sarcasm crystal clear. But not today. I had pitched my words sweetly, I'd looked her squarely in the eye and smiled genuinely, and something in her soul crumbled. Her lips began to move, but just as she prepared to deliver her witty retort the loudspeaker screeched on and Mr. Franklyn announced that he had started his rounds.

Booth number one was Maria's, so she rushed to take her place, losing her composure in the process. Her exposition, it was clear to see even from my remote vantage point, was not as confident as it usually was. She lost her train of thought once or twice and midway through the presentation I saw her father shake his head in disgust and leave the gym. Maria was devastated. She gamely finished up, but it was clear that the only person she had wanted to impress was no longer there. She wrapped up her talk and left the booth without answering any questions. The judges, clearly, were discombobulated. They moved on reluctantly.

Since I was in the nether regions of the gym I had a lot of time to rehearse my speech, but of course I forgot all of it by the time the judges finally arrived. The title to my booth was: 'A Nail-Biting Experience,' but the text of my poster, like the project itself, was covered. As the judges took their places, I pulled the covering away to reveal what I thought were elegant drawings of nail clippings catapulting into a bowl of cereal, hitting someone in the eye, or flying onto a dinner plate. The caption: 'Are you tired of unwanted projectiles? Then look no further. The Nail Catcher 5000 is for you!'

I made a big show of removing the cardboard box and revealing my invention. 'This is just a proof of concept. The design has to be refined. But my invention will rid the world of unwanted and lethal nail clippings.' I looked at Mrs. Munroe, the other science teacher. 'Tell me you aren't sick of your husband's toenail clippings flying through the air and landing where they don't belong.' She actually nodded. I waved at my tiny nail clipper, which I had encased in a giant transparent bubble. 'Voilà! Problem solved.'

Mr. Franklyn moved forward and placed his hand inside the bubble to grab the clipper. He reached his other hand into the small opening I'd made on the other side and he clipped his nail. A knife-sharp shard of nail flew straight at his defenceless eyeball, but it was safely intercepted by my plastic shield and the clipping fluttered harmlessly to the bottom of the catchment tray. I reached over to a part of my poster that was still covered and revealed the writing underneath. It read: 'Number of days without a fatal eye incident.' Underneath it, on the butcher's paper that I had stapled to it I wrote — **1** — with a great flourish of the blood-red marker. To my surprise the crowd burst into spontaneous applause, and one voice burst out above it all. 'That's my boy, *tabernacle!*' I looked into the audience and saw my father and mother standing there. I couldn't believe that he'd closed the store for this.

And when they put the cheap plastic trophy into my hands to celebrate my third-place finish, I honestly didn't care a bit. I was thrilled just to look out at the crowd and see my parents, smiling proudly as though I'd won the Stanley Cup. I looked over at Maria who stood there with the over-sized first place cup in her hands. The look on her face told me that she would have done anything to swap places with me that day and I felt bad for the way that I had misjudged her. Who knew a Science Fair could make you a better man? 'Hallelujah,' I thought, 'hallelujah.'

Sixteen

MAD MEN

I always loved writing and was an avid, perhaps even obsessive, reader. Which is why I was especially miffed when any English teacher approached the subject dispassionately. To have the privilege of teaching an incredible work of art and to make it feel like torture was a crime for which a suitably painful reprimand had not yet been devised. My English teacher was one of these, alas. She treated Shakespeare like a poisoned pill that she administered like a vaccination. No wonder then that everyone loathed his work. It was difficult, of course, especially for a high school audience, but it didn't need to be cancerous. To make matters worse, our teacher's name was Ms. Melville, and when I enthusiastically said, 'Like the person who wrote *Moby Dick*!' she sent me to principal's office for using offensive language. Even our dour principal was embarrassed about that one. 'Sit here for ten minutes and then go back to class looking sorry,' he said, and gave me a lollipop. I think I would have preferred the strap.

It's fair to say, therefore, that when the Vice-Principal announced that Ms. Melville would be away for the rest of the year, we were not at all sorry to inherit a young substitute teacher who looked like he had strayed from the set of an art-house movie. He had longish hair, wore jeans (which he was told in no uncertain terms he was not to do again), and he sat on, instead of behind, his desk. Truly, we had never seen anything cooler. Until he unveiled his plan for the rest of the semester. To begin, he explained, we would do a break-the-ice initiative which would help us to get to know our fellow classmates, that would teach us how to use language creatively, and which might also be a ton of fun at the same time. Who was this teacher and where had he been all my life?

'I want you to pick something you care about and write an ad campaign about it, though it has to reference *Romeo and Juliet* even if just remotely. This is your chance to use expressive language, to show your creativity, and to market something that you are passionate about. We'll use class time to develop our concepts, and then finish with a presentation to the class.' Other than the presentation part, everyone was pretty excited about the idea, if only because it meant Shakespeare was deferred until later in the term. We disbanded and spent the week thinking about what we wanted to do, and then we were called up to do a 'pitch' of our idea. 'Like the real Hollywood,' he said. 'Remember, there's no such thing as bad publicity.'

When it was my turn I decided I would swing for the fences. 'I think Shakespeare gets a bad rap, so I want to do an ad campaign that makes him cool. I wanted to take the most challenging product I could think of and see if I could make it work.' Our teacher, let's call him Mr. McCool, was nodding his head like crazy.

'Dude,' he said. 'That is an inspired idea. Like, brilliant. And it ties into the class syllabus, so the Vice-Principal won't fire me in week two. You rock, dude.'

I don't think higher praise had ever been given, and certainly not to me. The only sour note was Maria Vianetti, whose desk was closest to the teacher's, and who snickered when she heard my plan. I had had a bit of an insight into her character and developed some sympathies that explained her bullying, but that didn't make liking her any easier. She continued to be competitive and nasty, and as I returned to my seat she whispered, 'Good luck with your lame ass idea, dork.'

I was rattled, but not defeated, though I lost a bit of confidence when I heard her project. Maria was also head of the Radio Club, and so she proposed a campaign to advertise our local in-school station. 'It will be bold, punchy, and it will help with community spirit,' she explained. Mr. McCool just nodded his head and gave her the thumbs up. 'Community spirit!' he repeated, and Maria sashayed back to her seat like a marketing executive who had just scored the top client in the city. She had radio, I had Shakespeare. What was I thinking?

Later that day I sat in the outdoor yard of my father's store. It was filled with bags of concrete and soil, skips filled with construction products of one kind or another. I was perched on a large container of manure watching the neighbourhood dogs walking their owners, struggling to find an idea. And then it hit me. We were studying *Romeo and Juliet* and the edition we were using was Expurgated. I admit I didn't know what that meant, but I figured if my Catholic school was expurgating it, there had to be something it didn't want me to see. Thank God for the Public Library. It was hard work, but eventually I discovered all the naughty bits that were removed from our school edition. My ad, I thought, would market the most unmarketable product on the market — Shakespeare — and the marketing gods were smiling on me. They had given me the most marketable tool on the planet — sex. Literature and sexuality: that was my pitch. I was in my happy place.

'Are you sure that's a wise idea,' my father asked when I told him my plan. 'The school is pretty, ah, old school.'

'What's the worse they can do?' I asked.

'Fail you. Make you repeat the grade. Expel you. Force me to close the store and go in for an interview with that snooty principal.'

'Yeah, but, other than that.'

My father smiled. 'You got me there.' The great thing about my dad was that he never tried to bully you into accepting his point of view. I had never heard him raise his voice in anger, and he always brought people around to their better selves by appealing to their common sense. But he understood that sometimes there were multiple ways of doing things, and all of them could have merit. 'Well, whatever you decide to do, do it tastefully, and I'll have your back.'

'Thanks dad, I appreciate that.'

And so it was I began to work on my campaign. Mr. McCool allowed us to use the classroom to work on our posters, to read and research, and so the class itself was hopping. Kids were sharing markers, exchanging ideas, and talking excitedly. Occasionally a teacher from an adjacent class would come by to ask us to lower the volume, but then they'd stand there in shock at the energy in the room. Of course, the energy wasn't always positive. Maria inevitably came by my desk to mock my images and ridicule my concept (which mercifully I was keeping largely under wraps so that it wasn't shut down before I could present it). 'You see this,' she said pointing to her mouth, and then did an exaggerated yawn. 'That's what I think of your project.' And off she went.

Whenever I had the chance I made a point of dropping by the other desks, and it was exciting to trade ideas. When I went past Maria's hers consisted of a large poster with two columns. One side said, in huge colourful letters — 'Let's Get It On!' — and the other side had smaller messaging about the radio program content written in lowercase black lettering. The alternate column was where her struggle was. She was trying to find the right description for what the program did.

My project, on the other hand, was somewhat sleight of hand. I had the visible part, and then I planned to unveil the more risqué elements during the pitch. The way I explained it to myself was that version 'A' was the expurgated version, and version 'B' was unexpurgated. Censorship vs Freedom of Expression. My tag line was 'The Hidden Shakespeare.' When Mr. McCool saw this, and perhaps sensing something was amiss, he asked about the focus of the project. 'Ah, well, my argument is that if you don't understand Shakespeare, he remains hidden. Look at the kids in this class. No one wants to read him. So I want to show why he's relevant.' I pointed to the picture of Romeo and Juliet on the cover. 'They were our age, after all. This is about us.'

Mr. McCool nodded. 'Dude that's awesome. You almost make me want to read him.' And that was the only crack in his shiny armor. Otherwise, he 'dug' me. I was pretty sure that was a good thing.

As pitch day approached our projects were increasingly refined. I had quite a beautiful posterboard ready which I'd spent the weekend hand printing. Maria, pretending to innocently walk by, deliberately spilled a cup of water on my desk. 'I'm so sorry!' she exclaimed in a loud voice as the ink ran together on the poster. Everything was ruined. Mr. McCool rushed over and Maria turned on the tears: 'I don't know how it happened,' she cried, 'I was getting water for my brushes and just tripped. You should fail my project. Ban me from participating.' Mr. McCool, not quite so cool when a woman was crying, took her back to her desk and comforted her instead of me, then ran to fetch tissues from the teacher's lounge. While he was away Maria looked at me with a crooked smile: 'Oooops.' She started bawling as soon as he returned.

A couple of my friends came by and helped me mop up, but the damage was done. I would need to redo most of the artwork overnight in time for the pitch. 'Don't worry,' McCool assured me, 'I'll take this little mishap into consideration.'

Come pitch day Mr. McCool had arranged the room differently. He'd set things up like a small boardroom, so it had the look and feel of an Ad Agency. He had also inveigled a few teachers, and the Vice-Principal, to sit in on the pitch and be the 'clients' for the exercise. I have to admit, I hadn't expected that. But once the pitches started rolling, we all quickly forgot about our guests and got into the spirit of things. We tried to be supportive of each other, clapping especially loudly as each pitch was delivered. Maria, as one might expect, was the exception, loudly pointing out flaws. It was disconcerting because once or twice the 'judges' nodded when she criticized and then wrote in their notebooks.

As luck would have it, Maria and I were the last two. I'd had it with her meanness by the time she got up and decided to give her a taste of her own medicine if the opportunity arose. She placed her large board on the display tripod and unveiled it with a flourish. Her poster, professionally printed by her father's company, was glossy and slick. It had high quality images of radios and head-phones, cool looking microphones, Romeo and Juliet dancing, and of course a picture of Maria, wearing the headset, in the control room. The message consisted of two large columns of text side by side:

Let's Get   *Intimate and sensual*

It On!   *music to die for*

The impact of the production quality alone was extraordinary. The visiting committee of judges actually gasped audibly. It looked like a professional piece of work, and in fairness, given that her father produced these posters for a living, it didn't seem at all fair. Maria paused for one second too long before speaking and I saw my chance. In a loud, but friendly voice I said: 'I don't get it. "Let's get intimate and sensual?" Is that really appropriate for a high school radio station?'

Maria's face turned beet red. 'No! That's not what it says. That's not how you read it. Let's Get It On! Intimate and sensual music to die for! Romeo and Juliet die at the end....'

'This isn't Japan,' I said sweetly. 'We don't read top to bottom. We read left to right.'

'But you can see by the fonts,' she exclaimed, and then went on to do her pitch. The damage, though, was done. Once everyone read the text my way, they couldn't un-see it. Even the Vice-Principal was fighting to suppress a smile. One of the teachers actually snickered and lowered her head to hide her grin. The look on Maria's face, I must say, was worth the price of admission. Everyone applauded when she finished, but it was hard to tell what we were celebrating.

And then it was my turn. I carried my mangled poster board to the front of the room. To his credit Mr. McCool explained to the visiting delegates that I had dropped water on the poster the night before so they should be lenient when they judged the final product. Maria sniggered loudly for effect. I placed my poster on the tripod and removed the first covering:

The Hidden Shakespeare — Expurgated.

I displayed a large image of Romeo with Juliet chastely leaning across a balcony railing with select quotations from their speeches. I had put their ages underneath, and in brackets I wrote what grade they would be in if they attended our high school. The students legitimately gasped when they saw this. 'Oh my God,' someone called out, 'she's my age. That's so cool.' My buddy Karl said: 'I thought this was a play about old people. Like twenty-year-olds.' Everyone was chatting then, and the committee were visibly impressed. They were nodding at each other, writing enthusiastically in their notepads. Maria was apoplectic. Of course, she needn't have worried. I still had part two to unveil.

I pulled a piece of paper away and it showed a picture of our textbook with the word 'Expurgated' highlighted. I had the definition written next to it: 'a text where language or content, deemed rude or offensive, has been removed.' The Vice-Principal fidgeted uncomfortably and looked towards my teacher, who promptly looked out the window.

Then I pulled another sheet away from the second half of my display. It read:

The <u>real</u> Shakespeare — <u>Un</u>expurgated

Beneath the words I'd drawn an image of Mercutio and the Nurse. I'd drawn Mercutio with his lower body on a little spring so that his hips gyrated when I tapped the poster. And beside this I had the definition of 'Unexpurgated' — 'a text that is uncensored, as the author intended it to be.' I had quotes from the play with explanations: the death scene where Juliet grabs Romeo's dagger and plunges it into her body and says, 'O Happy dagger! This is thy sheath! Let it rust and die in me.' Next to it I had written: 'Dagger: metaphor for a man's private bits. Sheath: Latin for a woman's lady parts.'

In another square I had a conversation between Romeo and his friend Mercutio. The word bubble from Romeo read: 'Is love a tender thing? It is too rough,/ too rude, too boisterous, and it pricks like thorn.' Mercutio's response: 'If love be rough with you, be rough with love;/ Prick love for pricking, and you beat love down.'

I didn't bother translating that one. I also had one section of my poster explaining all of the rudest parts of the Nurse's dialogue, which was basically everything she said.

'Shakespeare,' I finished with a flourish, 'Is one of the greatest writers in history, but he was writing for everyday people, not fancy teachers. He used colourful language to keep his audience interested. So my message to you is, don't read censored Shakespeare, read the unexpurgated Shakespeare. And then go to Confession.' To say that the students were thrilled by my presentation is an understatement. Everyone was whooping and hollering, so much so that we couldn't hear what the Vice-Principal was saying as he stormed to the front of the room and threw my poster to the ground. Everyone fell into shocked silence. He pointed at me: 'I'll see you after school. Your father is going to hear about this!'

He left the room, slamming the door loudly, and everyone sat there stunned. Even Mr. McCool wasn't sure what to say. Finally, Maria, bless her competitive heart, raised her hand shakily. 'Did I win?' she asked.

Mr. McCool, looking decidedly uncool, turned to the remaining delegates. Ms. Sparks, who taught Home Economics, stood up slowly. She wasn't quite sure what to do either. 'I – I think we will reserve our decision for a later time. When we've had a chance to … review our notes.' With that the group stood awkwardly and left the classroom. We were still all sitting in silence when the loudspeaker squawked to life. It was the Vice-Principal, summoning me to the main office.

Well, I thought, from a marketing perspective, no one could say my work had gone unnoticed. As I prepared to leave, I turned to face the class and with a show of bravado that I didn't at all feel I announced: 'There's no such thing as bad publicity. Right?'

Mr. McCool was nodding. 'I certainly hope that's true,' he said at last. 'I certainly hope that's true.'

Seventeen

THE SPANISH INQUISITION

My parents weren't formally educated. Both were poor and had left school in fifth grade to help support their large families. Despite this my mother was a voracious reader. She loved to write poetry and read almost a book a day. My father, for his part, was a math savant. He could process numbers in his head like a calculator. When the travelling salesmen tried to bamboozle him with special orders and fake discounts, he could run rings around them, calculating the percentages down to the smallest decimal point.

Perhaps because of their lack of formal education, my parents were intimidated by places of learning, and being summoned to the principal's office at my high school to discuss their son's misdeeds made them particularly uncomfortable. I had dared to challenge the censorship gods and my exposé of Shakespeare's bawdy language had landed me in hot water. I was being charged with obscenity. I had discussed my presentation ahead of time with my father and he had advised me to be discreet, which I felt I had been. But the censorship board disagreed. To make matters worse, my dad had to close the store to attend the meeting, a loss of income that we could ill afford.

Nevertheless, we made our way to the school and perched in a shabby waiting room. There were only two chairs so I stood nervously by the corner window. When Mr. Chavez finally appeared it was with an imperious and hostile manner. He led us into his office where he spent an inordinate amount of time opening and reviewing my file, without so much as acknowledging my parents. I knew my dad. He would view this as disrespecting my mother, and that he never allowed. After the longest time, Mr. Chavez sighed melodramatically and looked up. 'I suppose you know why I called you here?' he said.

'Presumably,' my father responded smoothly, and despite his difficulty with English, which he'd slowly learned from my mother, he mimicked the principal's tone of voice with uncanny precision. 'Presumably it is because the school has a problem with Shakespeare.'

The principal wasn't expecting that response. 'Excuse me? What do you mean?'

'Well, my son did a presentation on Shakespeare, and here he is in trouble.'

'That is not why....'

'Shakespeare is part of the English canon, *non*?'

Mr. Chavez was completely disorientated. 'Yes of course he is. He's a classic.'

'And yet?' my father said.

'Your son is here because he defiled Shakespeare.'

My father turned to me in mock confusion. 'Defiled?'

I shrugged innocently. 'Raped? Ravaged? Had sex with?'

'No not that,' Principal Chavez interjected brusquely. 'He misrepresented Shakespeare to the class.'

'Ah. My son said things that were not true about the writing. What was the play?'

'*Romeo and Juliet*,' I said, helpfully.

'*Ah je vois*,' he said. 'That's the play about the two barely fourteen-year-old kids who want to get married. *Non?*' I was glad I'd briefed my dad on the way over. 'I see what you mean, monsieur principal.' He looked at me with mock anger. 'How dare you bring that kind of book to class.'

'No, it was a set text in the course,' Mr. Chavez explained defensively, his Spanish accent starting to come out as he got increasingly flustered.

'Wait. So the school, filled with fourteen-year-old kids, purposefully set a play about child marriage and suicide for children of the same age to read? *Mon dieu!*'

'Sir, you are missing the point.'

My father was on a roll, still annoyed at how the principal had treated my mum. 'And my son celebrated this I suppose. Like a sex maniac?'

'What? No.'

'Then my son said things that weren't true about Mr. Shakespeare's work?'

'What? No. But....'

My father adopted a confused tone. 'So he told the truth about the play?'

'He used inappropriate language,' Chavez snapped, and my father feigned disgust.

'You used a rude word?' my father said to me.

'Latin,' I responded, eyes laser-focused at my shoes. 'I explained the Latin meaning of a word.'

My father paused dramatically. 'But Latin is sophisticated. Academic, *non*? As a Spanish man you should know that.'

Mr. Chavez nearly exploded. 'He used the Latin word for vagina!' he screamed, and my mother gasped. Chavez looked mortified. 'Oh dear! I'm so sorry, I didn't mean....' My mother was not an actress, but I was quite sure she exaggerated the impact that the word had had on her finer sensibilities.

'Really, Mr. Chavez, was that necessary?' my father asked, patting my mother on her delicate arm. To her he whispered, though loud enough for all of us to hear, 'Perhaps you should have waited in the car,' neglecting the fact that we had walked to the school.

'But your son,' Mr. Chavez started to say, trying to rescue the moment.

'I didn't use that word, sir. I wrote 'lady parts' on my poster. My father told me to be polite at all times.'

'He used an inappropriate *edition* of Shakespeare,' Chavez corrected somewhat desperately through gritted teeth, starting to sound rather frantic.

'The expur-....' My father looked to me for help.

'I used an *un*expurgated edition.'

'*Ah, voilà.* You mean the one you borrowed from the public library?'

'*C'est ça,*' I said, deliberately switching to French.

My father turned a benign glance at the principal and his face lit up as though everything had suddenly become clear. 'I understand now! You have called me here because you want me to join the school board to lodge a complaint against the city for allowing … unexpurgated books to be loaned to young people?' If my father's English was hesitant at the best of times it seemed to be getting more confident by the minute. 'I'll do it, *bon dieu*! This is an outrage.'

Mr. Chavez looked ill. He sat back in his chair and shut the file. 'In retrospect, it seems to me that this is a complete misunderstanding.'

'*Ah oui*?' my father said. His innocent tone was hilarious. It took all my will power not to laugh. 'But my son has a black mark now on his record.'

Chavez shook his head. 'No, no, we will make sure it is removed.'

'So you will … *expurgate* his record,' my father said, emphasizing the word. Mr. Chavez's face turned a deep purple. He had looked uncomfortable before, but a wave of fury was washing over him now. Before he could say anything though my mother spoke up.

'So how is *Mrs.* Chavez?' she asked, her radiant smile filling the room.

Chavez was completely thrown. 'Excuse me? Yes. No. She is well. Thank you for asking.'

'Well, let's go,' my father said, standing abruptly. 'We've taken enough of the principal's valuable time. It was good to meet you.' With that he left the room and we hurried after him. I wondered, though, how Mr. Chavez would explain the meeting to his team. Outside in the cool evening air every sound seemed magnified. I felt terrible, but my father had a twinkle in his eye.

'Dad, I'm *so* sorry I made you close the store for this.'

He shrugged. 'You know, it does us good to get out once in a while. I think we should take your delicate mother out to her favourite Chinese restaurant to help her recover from all that vulgarity. What do you say?'

My mother laughed and squeezed his arm. 'Your son says "yes". Otherwise *he'll* be in unexpurgated trouble.'

Eighteen

TOO MCCOOL FOR SCHOOL

When I returned to my English class after my brief absence, I was mortified to discover that Mr. McCool, the best teacher I'd ever known, had been replaced. I felt absolutely gutted knowing that my small presentation on Sex and Shakespeare had got him fired. To make matters worse, Maria **Vianetti** was sitting in the front row with a smile as wide as the Grand Canyon on her face, and a blue First Place certificate on her desk. She had clearly won the marketing competition that Mr. McCool had set, which I had nearly been suspended over.

As I walked past her desk she mumbled, 'I'm surprised to see you here,' but not with the venom that she usually reserved for me. 'Did you stick it to the man?'

I paused by her desk. 'Not me. My father did. No one messes with my dad.'

She looked genuinely pleased for me. 'Good for you. For what it's worth, I thought your presentation was really brave. I'm sorry I almost ruined it.'

I wasn't sure who this person was, but I wasn't going to take this peace for granted. 'You know what, the rough and tumble look actually suited the work. Made it more authentic.'

She laughed. 'Anything I can do to help.'

I wanted to keep the détente going: 'Your dad will be thrilled about your award.'

Maria's face darkened. 'He won't care about a stupid ribbon. He just wants me to win. That's all that matters in our family. Nobody is allowed to lose.'

I didn't know what to say to that, but I remembered her father's face during the Science Fair when she had briefly lost her train of thought. He had looked disgusted, and he had stormed from the gym. If my mother had a fault, it was that she went the opposite way. I could do no wrong. If I brought home a poor result, she celebrated it as though I'd split the atom. For some reason that I don't fully understand now, I was always incensed by her support. I went out of my way to explain to her why I was mediocre. When I did, she would hug me so lovingly it was painful. 'Oh honey, you're such a funny boy.' Now, watching Maria's face I thought how sad it was that she didn't have that kind of approval. I hadn't realized how much it had meant to me.

My train of thought was interrupted by the arrival of the substitute-substitute teacher. The Vice-Principal brought her in himself and introduced her to the class, but although he addressed us all, his eyes were fixed on me. He explained that this was her first teaching gig, and that she was a prized former student of the school itself, and there would be hell to pay if she wasn't treated with the utmost respect. 'So make her welcome, and behave.'

Ms. McDonald was an astonishingly beautiful woman, very prim, and clearly nervous to be teaching her first class. 'So, kids,' she said to us, 'we need to catch up on where you are.'

I raised my hand. 'We're studying *Romeo and Juliet*,' I volunteered helpfully.

Ms. McDonald looked incredibly uncomfortable. 'Well, about that. It seems that the book has been replaced. Unsuitable, apparently.' Needless to say, there was a fair bit of commotion. We'd already forked out money to buy the book, and while few had actually read it, we all acted as though we'd invested hours studying the text. And since I had done a presentation focusing on all the naughty bits in the play, a few of my fellow students were actually keen to find them. 'It's not appropriate,' she repeated, and held up another Shakespeare play. 'We'll be doing *Richard the Third*.'

I raised my hand helpfully. I hadn't actually studied the play but had read a detailed summary of the plot when I was preparing my earlier presentation. 'We're replacing a play about under-aged children getting married with a play about a guy who kills tons of people, forces one of his murder victim's wives to marry him and then kills a couple of kids for good measure? That's more appropriate?'

Ms. McDonald smiled at me. She was truly, incredibly, beautiful. 'Since you know so much about it,' she said sweetly, and my heart melted. I was hers for all eternity. I was prepared to marry her on the spot. 'You can do the first presentation next week.' She turned demurely towards her desk and asked us to take out our notebooks. Then she began to conjugate verbs on the blackboard.

Mr. McCool would never have stooped to teaching us grammar. It was torture, plain and simple. I wanted a divorce.

As soon as class was over Maria turned sharply towards me. 'Because of you, we have to study a play that's three times longer. Idiot!' She stormed from the room. The ceasefire was clearly over.

I headed home morosely, the library copy of *Richard the Third* tucked uncomfortably under my arm. I had read somewhere that Shakespeare's character was one of the most despicable, distorted and horrific human beings ever created, but even that didn't cheer me up. I had to do a presentation on him with just over a week to go. I comforted myself with the fantasy that I might receive some private lessons from Ms. McDonald, but when I got home, I saw just how hefty the work actually was. Maria was right. I was an idiot. I had gotten a beloved teacher fired, and I'd forced everyone to read what turned out to be an impossibly difficult play.

I also knew that I until my presentation was over, I had to spend less time around my father. Although I was learning to disguise my French accent, so that at times my English was flawless, in times of stress certain pronunciation errors would reappear. The hardest thing to master, as a French speaker, was the 'th' sound. If I was speaking quickly or inattentively, the hard 'd' sound took over. 'De water in de bucket is frozen.' If I got nervous, my tongue refused to cooperate. And nothing made me more uncomfortable than public speaking.

The play was tough. Impossibly difficult. Elizabethan English was not for the faint of heart and especially not for the typical teenager. Even a native English speaker would struggle. On top of that, I began to have dreams about Mr. McCool. In one of them I saw him in a shelter, teaching grammar to fellow homeless people. It didn't seem particularly realistic that the homeless would trade soup and buns to learn how to conjugate a verb, but the point of my dreams was surely not realism. Instead, night after night I imagined my former teacher in an increasingly hopeless predicament, struggling to feed himself now that he was destitute. In one particularly brutal dream I actually became Richard the Third himself, heartlessly locking Mr. McCool in the Tower of London. It was all too much.

On the fateful day of my presentation, I appeared miserably at the class only to be confronted by the Vice-Principal himself. 'Show me your bag?' he barked. 'Are you planning anything … inappropriate?' he scowled.

'No sir!' I shouted, parodying a military cadet answering his sergeant.

'Watch this one closely,' he said to Ms. McDonald. He left, still scowling. She tried to be comforting, but the combination of all the factors had me rattled. I was forgetting some of my English words. When it came time I was summoned to stand in front of the class. Maria was scowling at me, the class was visibly, excruciatingly bored, and even Ms. McDonald's extraordinary face did not cheer me up. I could feel my palms dripping sweat. And even though I heard my French overwhelming my practiced English pronunciation, I knew I couldn't stop it.

'Today I am doing a presentation on Richard de Turd.' The laughter was instantaneous. I looked over at Ms. McDonald. She had her head in her hands. I soldiered on. I can't recall what I said, and I know it wasn't brilliant, but I rushed through my notes, called for questions, and then promptly sat down.

'Well,' Ms. McDonald began, 'I don't know what to say.' She turned towards the blackboard and began to conjugate verbs as though she was possessed. Somehow, this time, I was relieved.

That afternoon, still feeling miserable that I had cost Mr. McCool his job, but now with the added weight of my disastrous presentation, I took the long way home. I headed into the small shopping district on main street. As I walked past the local ski shop, I saw Mr. McCool behind the counter. My heart broke to see him there. I couldn't walk past without apologizing. I took a minute to build up my nerve and then pushed through the shop entrance and moved towards his counter. I wasn't sure what I would say and almost turned around. Just then he raised his head and saw me. To my surprise his face lit up: 'Dude! How are you?'

It was one thing to cost someone their job, but quite another for them to be nice to me afterwards. 'Sir,' I gushed, 'I am so sorry that my stupid presentation got you fired.'

He looked genuinely surprised. 'Dude, chill. You didn't get me fired. Your courageous attack on hypocrisy inspired me. I thought to myself, if that little dude can stand up to the establishment, then I have no excuse to stay here and let it suck my soul dry. So, I left.'

'I didn't get you fired?'

'Dude, you liberated me.' I didn't know what to say. The store was filling up and I could see that he had to go. 'Just so you know,' I said before he could rush off. 'You're the best teacher I ever had. Because of you I want to become an English professor.'

He was nodding. 'Respect, dude. Always call it like it is. Deal?'

'You got it,' I said. 'Shakespeare: sex, drugs and rock'n'roll.'

He slapped my back. 'Rock on, dude. The bard would be proud.'

Nineteen

MY LITERARY CAREER

Thanks to Mr. McCool, I realized that my passion for reading could be seriously explored in a classroom and I managed to talk my way into an advanced Canadian literature course. In part they were desperate to have enough students to run it, and in part it was because one of the judges in my unexpurgated Shakespeare class was another hippie teacher who I later learned loved my presentation. At the time, I assumed it was because the content was so avant-garde, cutting-edge, trailblazing, pioneering and ahead of its time, but it turns out she hated the Vice-Principal and anything that got under his skin suited her just fine.

Because I'd been in an advanced program in elementary school, they allowed me to join the class 'in progress' for extra credit and I quickly found that I was ridiculously behind everyone from the get-go.

'Are you sure you can do this?' Ms. Joy asked. 'I don't take any prisoners. Sink or swim in my classes, baby.'

Not much of a laid-back hippie, I thought using my inside voice. 'No problem,' I replied using my outside voice, but no longer quite so confident. 'I'm a fast reader, Ms. Joy,' I added, thinking, boy, you were misnamed. Pretty sure that was my inside voice as well, though judging by the sour look on Ms. Joyless's face, I was no longer certain.

'Okay, then. Read this for tomorrow.' She handed me a set of badly photocopied sheets. 'Short stories.'

Awesome, I thought. What's a few pages? I've got this. I tucked them away in my backpack and headed off to my last class. This was followed by gym practice, then a long walk home. One of my cranky aunts dropped by unannounced so I was forced to socialize. One thing led to another, as they say, and I forgot to do the readings.

The next morning, in between classes, I realized that I no longer had a free period. I gathered up my backpack and rushed to class, and in the process realized I hadn't done the reading. I ran into the classroom and took my seat. Joyless was writing on the board and didn't turn around. 'You're late. That's not happening again? Are we clear?'

'Yes Miss!' I responded, and then frantically fished the photocopies out of my bag. I spread them on the desk and my dislike of Stephen Leacock was born that day. I had never heard of him before, but in a blind panic, hoping I could secretly read his story before the teacher finished her epic work on the blackboard, I dove in. Unfortunately for me, the story was 'My Financial Career,' and I began giggling from the first paragraph. By the second paragraph I was struggling to contain a belly laugh. And by the end of the story I was rolling in the aisle — almost literally. I had so much water in my eyes I was afraid they'd hook me up to the sprinkler system.

Without turning around Ms. Joyless announced to the class, 'Well someone didn't do the readings.' I pushed the story away and mopped at my eyes. I wanted to be worried but the words of the character in the story kept popping back into my head, so that I couldn't stop laughing. Even on the verge of expulsion, Leacock was intent on sabotaging my burgeoning academic career. It was unfair.

Joyless put down the chalk and walked to the front of the class. She pointed at me. 'That!' she said. 'That is what literature can do!' She surveyed the room. She was nodding. 'You guys didn't read it either, did you?' I'd never before seen so many heads snap down all at once. The synchronization was actually rather impressive. Her head kept sweeping the room, back and forth, back and forth. No one said a word. I put up my hand.

'I think we should read it together out loud. Anything this funny should be shared. And boy does it make me want to read the other things on the class reading list … now that I've seen how impeccable your taste in literature is.'

Joyless fixed me with her glare. 'Excruciatingly lame flattery will not work in this class, young man, nor in the real world. But I like your idea. Leacock should be shared. Let's do it. But you're reading.'

I was already shaking my head. 'I can't! I barely got through it the first time.'

'All the more reason for you to do it.'

'Okay,' I answered, 'but if I pee my pants I'm blaming you.'

'Hah!' Her laugh, when it exploded out of her, was like a one note detonation, and then it was over. 'I'll risk it. Start reading.'

Unlike my disastrous experience presenting on Shakespeare aloud, my English didn't falter, and as I read and became hysterical, everyone quickly got into it, laughing along with me. It took ten times longer to read it because we kept having to stop and catch our breath, but it was the first time I had seen words move an audience and make a connection. Someone actually asked us to read another one of his stories, 'Gertrude the Governess,' which we did. I fell in love with Leacock that day.

After class the teacher asked me to hang back. The students filed out, a few actually smiling at me as they left. When the last person had gone I turned to her quickly.

'Miss, I'm sorry about the story. I'm just trying to get used to the new schedule.'

She put her hand up. 'No apology necessary, but obviously don't do it again. Still, good job today. You really helped to make the words come alive. That matters.'

I didn't know what to say. Perhaps she wasn't as Joyless as I thought. She looked at me oddly, as though she was suddenly surprised to see me there. 'Well? Get out of here? I've got another class to teach.'

'Yes Miss,' I answered, 'I'll hop on my bike and ride off in all directions at once.'

'Don't misquote Leacock,' she said mock-seriously, 'it's sacrilegious.'

I nodded. I was going to like this class.

'I certainly hope so,' Joyless replied.

Okay, I thought, I must have used my outside voice just then.

Twenty

THE BABYSITTER

It was extremely rare for my parents to go out. If they did, they almost always brought me with them. So, when they announced that they had an exciting evening planned with some friends I was rather shocked. My father appeared from the bedroom sporting a neat black suit jacket which I'd only ever seen him wear to funerals. He had on a crisp white a shirt, a dark blue tie, and he had shaved and then scrubbed the hardware store right off his hands — no mean feat considering the amount of grease and oil he handled daily. I was shocked.

'You look....' I started to say.

'Handsome!' my mother purred.

'I was going to say alien, but okay.'

'I spoke to J.P.'s mother and her niece, Katherine, has agreed to baby....'

My father cut her off quickly. 'She needs a bit of money, so we thought we'd help her out. Pretend you needed someone to stay with you while we're out.'

I wasn't born yesterday. I could see what was happening. 'Out of the question!' I exclaimed, incensed that they thought I needed babysitting. 'I'm perfectly fine to stay on my own. I'm a working man....'

'We may be quite late,' my mother cajoled, 'and I won't be able to relax if I'm worried about you the whole time. It's not you, it's me.'

I was about to protest but the doorbell rang, and my mother rushed to answer, happy to get away. I was staring daggers at my dad, and he was fidgeting uncomfortably. He knew very well that he had broken the bro' code. I wasn't going to let him off the hook. 'I can't believe you'd do this....' Before I could finish my sentence, my mother entered the kitchen with Katherine. To my amazement the babysitter was absolutely stunning ... for an older woman. She looked at least twenty.

My father saw immediately that she had caught my eye. 'You were saying, son?' he asked mischievously, and in English, which told me that my babysitter only spoke French.

'Nothing,' I stammered distractedly. 'If you are helping some-one in need, what kind of man would I be to object.'

'Well, that's very noble of you,' he chuckled. 'Although there's still time to cancel.' Since I didn't respond he crossed the room and shook Katherine's hand. He listened impatiently as my mother went through a laundry list of instructions. She ended by saying that all the details were on the fridge. 'Then why did you just spend all that time explaining?' he asked in frustration.

Katherine laughed. 'It's quite all right. It helps to hear what you expect of me. But honestly, we'll be fine.' She looked at me and

PART THREE

In which our hero dedicates his life to the service of women

Twenty-one

GRAY'S ANATOMY

I hope no one will judge me poorly if I admit that once I entered junior high, and prompted by my close encounter with a babysitter, I decided to switch my service from the Church to a concentration on women. My thinking at the time was simple: I had already done so much to help the parish forge a dynamic path with young people; wasn't it only fair that I offer the same service to womankind? It may seem counter-intuitive, but really, when you got right down to it, one was a natural extension of the other. The Church was obsessed with sexuality; and I was desperately in search of mine. Win-win.

That is not to say that I was not initially baffled by the transition, because I certainly was. Firstly, I was plagued by guilt. How would Fr. Rémi manage the parish without me? For that matter, how could inter-religious harmony succeed without the earnest translator that I had become? Not to mention the impact I'd had on Church music and publishing. Secondly ... well, there was no second. I just felt guilty. My father wisely told me that Catholics had perfected guilt. I didn't want to let him down, so I tried to be miserable whenever I could.

131

It is perhaps also true to say, however, that the Church had introduced me to the concept of Forbidden Fruit, and in my neighbourhood the thinking was, if you don't want boys to be interested in something, don't bring it up. Clearly the Church, despite my best efforts, did not agree with this philosophy. Every second homily seemed to be about sex; the ten commandments in my school had been replaced with the ten 'Don'ts', and all of these had something to do with an interest in the opposite sex.

To say that the parish priest was devastated when I stopped helping him on his mission would be to stretch the truth somewhat … well, entirely. Despite years of persistent service Fr. Rémi occasionally asked me who I was. Well, his wording was more specific — 'Who do you think you are?' — but you get the point. But just because I personally understood the causal relationship between my early near-priestly service and my raging hormones, I also knew enough to keep those urges to myself. Adults, I was beginning to see, were quite skilled at ruining youthful plans. How many times had my mother swooped in unreasonably to stop me from setting fire to the gas cannisters in the back yard — in the name of science — or prevented me from tethering my bike to a passing pick-up truck? The answer: too often. So how could I expect sound, liberal-minded support about the opposite sex from anyone heading towards extinction and entering their forties.

I had two best friends: one was J.P., my neighbourhood pal; and Karl Gunter, my English-speaking bestie at the English school. Neither could speak the other's language, so if they ever met, which was rare, they simply glowered at each other; but despite this linguistic divide each was as clueless and disinterested about the opposite sex as the other, despite J.P.'s early promise. I had no one. It was with grim determination that I realized I had to forge my own path and had to tackle this quest on my own. Thus were all the great sagas undertaken. The Greek warrior Odysseus battling Cyclops, Hercules and his Twelve Labours, Dante's descent into hell, Mickey Fitzbottom visiting the girls' locker room dressed only in a diaper. All these heroes had braved death alone and lived to tell the tale: well except Mickey who had a gag order imposed on him, so he never actually said a thing.

If I was going to get anywhere on my quest to become a true Romeo, though preferably one who didn't die, I would have to travel it on my own. I would have to seek the answers in our culture's deepest corners, confront the knowledge-keepers at their base. So I went to the school counsellor. Why I thought a guy called Slomo Bundengelder could help with this is beyond me, but at the time my frame of reference was limited. And Slomo was rumoured to have talked a kid into committing suicide. Admittedly not the usual goal, but counter-intuitive in a way that might prove useful. I didn't want an establishment message — I wanted ground-penetrating radar.

The school counsellor's office was in an awkward part of the building, down from the principal's office and wedged beside the cafeteria. Anyone using his services didn't want to be seen by either because of the associated stigma. The counsellor at our school was also not a highly sought position. I only knew this because I'd once stumbled into the teacher's lounge and four people were pushing the counsellor's plaque back and forth between them: 'You do it,'

'No you do it.' 'I don't want to.' 'I'll do the washing up for the month if you take it on.'

Entering Slomo's office didn't exactly instill you with confidence either. On the wall above his desk there were two certificates. One was a teaching diploma, the other a parchment saying, 'I did 40 hours at the ACME school of hard knocks, and I survived to tell the tale.' I may be misremembering the wording just a bit, but it was obviously forgettable. In any event, I was low on options, so I appeared at my designated hour and sat in the lumpy seat opposite the counsellor's desk. After a time, Slomo — sorry, Mr. Bundengelder — arrived.

'So young man,' he said, then spilled his coffee all over his desk. 'Shit! Hang on, will you?' He rushed from the room and returned with a wad of toilet paper. He made a valiant effort at mopping up the mess and then sat, in what I imagined was supposed to be a nonchalant manner, on the edge of the desk. I watched as the coffee seeped into his trousers, but he didn't seem to notice. 'So, what can I help you with today?' He picked up his coffee mug and sipped at what had to be the dregs that remained.

'I want to know how I can have meaningful intracorpse with the opposing sex,' I announced, misremembering the terms.

To his credit Slomo managed to project the meager dregs of his coffee a fair distance, covering me in a sticky residue. 'What?'

'I want to…' I repeated but he held up his hand.

'I know what you said. What do you *mean* though? You're a minor.'

'A minor what?' I asked. I'd been called a major pain before, so I wanted to understand if I was being demoted in any way.

'You're underage!'

I was getting frustrated. 'Under *what* age?' And then, seeing a glimmer of hope, I winked. 'Oooh. The Age of Enlightenment. I got you.'

'Wha? No. Dude. You're a kid. Kids don't have sex.'

'What about Billy the Kid, Kid Curry, the Sundance Kid...?'

'Are you messing with me? Did Shelley send you in here to mess with me?'

'Who's Shelley? And no. I just want some help. I dedicated my youth to the church and now, I think I want to have greener pastures. *Esprit de corps*,' I added, jazzing it up with some French. 'Emphasis on the *corps*.'

Slomo stared at me in silence. Then his head began to nod, faster and faster. 'I see. Yes, I see.' He stood and I couldn't help but stare at the large dark coffee stain that ran from his buttocks to his mid-thigh. He moved towards a filing cabinet and began to rifle through one of the drawers. He was actually cackling. 'Yup. This is it!' he muttered, more to himself than for my benefit. He gathered a bunch of flyers together and then put them in an envelope. He made a big show of sealing the envelope before handing it over to me. 'You sure Shelley didn't...?' He looked at my face. He could see I was in earnest. 'Okay then. This is all you need to know.' He said this with an expression on his face that was at once creepy and self-satisfied. 'Use it wisely. Don't tell anyone who gave it to you. Deal?'

'Yes,' I said.

'Great. Now off you go. Don't read this at school though. Promise me you'll find a secluded spot and study this carefully.'

I was beginning to get excited. 'You bet.' With that he gently pushed me out of the room and shut the door.

The three hours left of school followed by choir practice were hell. All I could think about was the timebomb in the sealed envelope burning a hole in my backpack. As soon as I could I ran all the way home, and feigning a stomach-ache, I skipped dinner and retreated to my room. My hand was trembling as I tore the envelope open. I have to admit, what I found was not at all what I expected, and my expectations were pretty ambiguous. I couldn't tell if this was an act of madness or genius.

Inside the envelope, Slomo had gathered graphic pamphlets on every type of sexually transmittable disease known to humankind, including a few that surely were made up. I discarded the one on leprosy but wasn't sure about the rest. I learned a new vocabulary that evening. I know he was trying to frighten me off my quest, but the images were explicit. Like nothing I'd ever seen before, including in the *Gray's Anatomy* textbook that I'd briefly consulted in the school library before the head librarian had taken it away from me and put it in the Restricted Material section. Read a certain way, the pamphlets were arguably a how-to guide, explaining things about the human body that I hadn't quite understood before.

I studied the pictures carefully and then returned them to the envelope. I had definitely misjudged him. Somehow, Slomo had both expanded and narrowed my horizons at the same time. I knew more about something that I completely failed to understand, and I was more certain of my confusion than ever before. If the jury was out before it had now resoundingly rendered its verdict: Slomo Bundengelder was an unmitigated genius.

Twenty-two

DEATH OF A LADIES' MAN

Not long after my meeting with the school counsellor, I came across a serendipitous find that quite literally changed my life and turned me into the suave, sophisticated man of the world that I am today. There, in a box of old books and comics that I had bought at an estate rummage sale, was a discarded copy of *Playboy* magazine. This was not the era of the internet, so to say that the work revealed some quite unexpected information on the human form is an understatement, so to speak. And to see the human form in explicit detail without graphic skin ailments or leprosy was surprisingly refreshing. Few reading this will believe me when I say that what most impacted me were the articles. Eventually. In truth, perhaps only one. It was a groundbreaking, foolproof, money-back guaranteed guide to becoming a ladies' man.

It contained secrets about the law of the jungle. For example, never let her make the first move. It had tips on the secret power of eye contact, and about the weaker sex's endearing vulnerabilities that one could tap in order to swoop any woman off her feet. And it was guaranteed. So, I studied that guide. Where a shallower man might have busied himself studying two-dimensional pictures, I memorized the secrets that a benevolent and wise man of the world had graciously shared. Not for profit, I might add, but because that journalist knew how important it was that women have access to the stud muffin that I would inevitably become.

I decided to test some of the key secrets immediately. On my return to school on Monday morning, I approached a young lady who had long ago caught my fancy but who had always been characterized as 'out of my league.' To be fair, out of the 1000 or so girls at my comprehensive school, it had been made very clear to me that 999 were out of my league. But, I reasoned, that leaves one, somewhere, and I was sure the odds were greatly increased in my favour now that I was a ... well, ladies' man. So, I walked up to Anna Maria Rosa and struck the pose I was instructed to take. I wiggled my eyebrows up and down suggestively in what, I must confess, had looked ridiculous earlier when I tested it in front of the bathroom mirror. But the guide guaranteed success, so I wiggled those eyebrows.

To her credit, I could see Anna Maria struggling to resist me. Her face had an ineffable expression. Well, now that I look back, the expression was pretty effable. 'What's wrong with your face?' she asked, and, again to acknowledge the guide, she looked genuinely concerned. 'Do you want me to call the nurse? Are you having a seizure?'

'No, I'm not having a seizure,' I answered indignantly.

'Lint? Something in your eye?'

'No there's nothing in my eye...' and then I remembered the guidebook, 'Except your extraordinary beauty.'

Unfortunately, as I said this Anna Maria was taking a deep gulp from her soda and she snorted it right at me. 'I'm so sorry,' she said, clearly falling under my spell. 'You're so funny.'

I watched her walk away, my eyes twitching now because of the burning soda. Okay, I thought, that was good. Maybe I was too ambitious. Perhaps I should be unleashing this incredible power on ladies who don't know me, that way I am not forcing them to un-learn who I used to be … before this staggering transformation.

And so, at lunchtime, once I was sure the redness had mostly left my soda-covered eyes, I left the school grounds and walked to-wards the grocery store. It stood at the confluence of a number of different schools that could always be counted on to have a bevy of unattached beautiful women. I took my time. Confidence, the guide assured me, was a state of mind. Women, in the grip of a tru-ly confident aura, were apparently helpless. I must confess I felt guilty at the power I was about to unleash on an entirely unsus-pecting gender, but Darwin would have had no such qualms. I had to man up.

I waited until the right lady appeared. Sure enough, near the grocery carts, a vision of uncommon loveliness appeared out of the fast-food burger joint, accompanied by her grandmother. They were walking straight towards me. I squared my shoulders and ambled forward, eyebrows twitching in that irresistible manner that I'd perfected, and I phased out all distractions. My vision was laser-focused on the beautiful raven-haired woman who, I was quite sure, would be my bride … once I got my driver's license of course.

There is no doubt in my mind that she knew she was the chosen one. Her head tilted coquettishly to one side, one of her eyebrows folded down, confused at first, and then both rose, perhaps at the urging of her heartbeat, and then, just as we were about to pass it happened. I don't know how many of you have experienced walking into a waist-high bollard. I suspect it's unpleasant for most, but it has an especially dire consequence on the male anatomy. I was in the process of administering my coolest nod and eyebrow twitch to the beguiling young woman, just as the concrete barrier compressed my left testicle with the ferocity of a pit bull discovering its favourite steak.

Try as I might to keep my manly veneer intact, once the intense pain had travelled to my conscious brain I had little choice but to let out such a high-pitched shriek that I am quite certain I shattered the spectacles on my dream girl's grandmother's face. By the time I could breathe again, my true love and her now blinded grandmother were long gone.

Crestfallen — and yes that's a euphemism — I limped back to school for the remainder of my classes. Afterwards I was sitting on one of the swings in the now-empty schoolyard, too depressed to go home. It is one thing to fail at something new, but quite another to mess up a sure thing that is guaranteed to work, charitably written by what was no doubt one of the great minds of our time. My sense of hopelessness and my lack of self-worth were deep.

I was too absorbed in self-pity, I must admit, to notice when Miranda sat down on the swing next to me. 'How's it going?' she asked kindly, and when I looked up I noticed how beautiful and rather amazing this person, who had sat in almost all of my classes all term, suddenly looked to me. I briefly contemplated wriggling my eyebrow, but honestly everything in my body hurt. 'I think I have a broken testicle,' I blurted. As soon as I said it I knew I had just sealed my fate one more time. To my surprise she just laughed. 'Well, you have two.'

Let me be honest, I did not expect her comment, and I started to laugh. Then she did too. After a time, and against the very laws of nature she asked, 'Do you want to go get a soda?'

The wave of gratitude that washed over me in that moment is impossible to describe. 'Yes,' I said, very possibly holding back tears, 'yes I'd really like that.' When I tried to stand I almost doubled over in pain. 'Old war wound,' I whispered, at least an octave higher than my usual register.

'Do you want to go via the Emergency ward first?' she asked, genuinely concerned.

I shook my head. 'Not a chance. It's nothing that a soda can't fix.'

Twenty-three

FIELD OF DREAMS

I don't want to say that my obsession with becoming a ladies' man in school put me on the radar with the hot girls. Mostly — well entirely — because it hadn't. Unbeknownst to me, however, a competition was raging among the 'hot ones' to see who could initiate the greatest number of guys to 'first base'. A popular movie of the time had popularized the idea that guys never forgot their first kiss, and in their hubris, the 'hot ones' wanted to ensure their place in history. As I understood this, the initiative had very little to do with the actual game of baseball.

'It's a metaphor,' I explained sagely to my friend Karl. 'Where a woman runs around an empty field and gives her heart in stages to her future stud muffin.'

Karl looked unimpressed. 'Should have been a hockey metaphor, then,' he scowled. 'We're in bloody Canada.'

I tried to contain my condescension. 'Yes, but baseball is more … international. The *World* Series! Hello!'

And so it transpired that the hottest girl in school chose me as her great beloved. That day will forever be sealed in my heart —

when our eyes met, and she spoke those immortal words: 'You! You're next!' I don't want to overstate the impact, but when Marie-France Delormier fixed me with her cobalt blue eyes it was truly impossible to look away. I must confess, too, that I was a little bit terrified. There were thirty or so onlookers, so at least I had intimacy on my side, but still. What if I failed?

When my father jokingly called me a man of the world, I thought he meant that I had a globe on my desk. Nonetheless, I was sufficiently sophisticated to know a moment of grave opportunity when it presented itself, and as a soon to be thirteen-year-old, I was also the older man. So, I planted my feet firmly, one slightly behind the other to brace for the inevitable impact, and then watched as Marie-France's beautiful mouth approached mine, much as I imagined a rocket would approach a space station for docking. I tilted my head in anticipation of our inevitable collision. It was, I thought, like two jet planes coming towards each other — and indeed, when our lips eventually met there were sparks … from the impact of our braces grinding and then locking painfully together, with such force and passion I might add, that it would take a dentist and an EMS guy to separate us.

It was not how I imagined my first real kiss would be. We were literally stuck together surrounded by dozens of school kids, in what I can only imagine was an admiring audience. 'What a stud!' I was sure the guys were thinking. 'I hope he brushed his teeth,' someone actually said. In any event, there we were, locked at the mouth in what can only truthfully be called a painful embrace. It took a while for someone to notice and rush away to get medical support. As I waited I thought, 'well, maybe I should practice my technique.' So, being an entrepreneur even at such a young age, I flicked my lips forwards, ignoring the searing pain, in what I could only hope was a romantic tour-de-force. 'Mwaah, Mwaah!' My lips flickered like a groper's.

Marie-France's eyes registered confusion — and perhaps, let's be honest — momentary pleasure, before her pupils dilated even further. They were initially quite enlarged because our faces were so close together that there was very little light getting in. But suddenly, a fleck of anger appeared, and she whispered her first passionate words to me. 'Cut it out, you idiot!' Of course, we were joined at the lip so it sounded more like 'OOitoooteedeeeo,' which I interpreted as 'thank you.' Still, not wanting to overwhelm her with my prowess I pulled back from my amorous lip flicks, which itself caused us tremendous pain (parting can be such sweet sorrow and all that). My heart skipped a beat and caused such a strong stabbing pain to my chest that I thought I had grown an extra nipple. I am sure she saw me as a combination of the great lovers of TV and film: Cary Grant and Peppy LePew.

When the EMS and emergency services team — well the janitor — arrived, he wasn't sure at first how to handle the situation. A parent, who was also a dentist, was luckily on hand and tried to explain the situation. At one stage we had so many hands trying to navigate our mouths that I felt we were in a piano recital. I wondered briefly if my luck would have been different if I'd been chosen by Marie-France's main rival, but then I remembered that her braces were big enough to support the Canadian Pacific Railway. Marie-France was indeed the fortunate one.

When at last we were separated, in what I can only imagine sounded like the screeching of two ships rubbing together in a late night collision at the docks, the onlookers applauded loudly. I knew that an important rite of passage had been completed. Marie-France, I could tell, felt the same. She looked at me with tear-filled eyes and her slightly bruised lips started to form the words I'd been waiting to hear. 'You asshole!' she cried, though because her braces were dislodged in her mouth, so that it looked very much like she was chewing on a couple of silver caterpillars, the words sounded, somehow, romantic. In a heavy metal, demented kind of way.

I tried to smile in a debonair manner, but it was difficult because my own braces were now perpendicular to my mouth. And despite my friends high-fiving me for my Olympic feat, I felt wistful to see her go. In a remarkable way it occurred to me that they were right. As fleeting as this was, I would indeed remember my first kiss forever. Who can say why? Later, Karl would proudly tell anyone who would listen that, 'He kissed her for 20 minutes!'

'Did he breathe?' someone asked.

'Not once!' Karl proudly confirmed.

Yes, I was now the school Casanova for sure, though I secretly vowed never to abuse my newfound status. In reality, however, I thought to myself, 'If this is how hard it is to get to first base, then I am never playing baseball again.'

Twenty-four

THE SOUND OF MUSIC

My high school was made up of three main student groups: the majority English kids, and then French and Italians in equal numbers. A small minority of kids were Asian: the children of Chinese and Filipino migrants. To say that we respected these boundaries is an understatement. The French kids always bonded together to fight the Italian kids, unless our beef was with the English kids. Then the Italians and the French were permitted to work together. It was a question of numbers. A science really.

It was rare indeed that the Asian kids entered into the equation, especially on the battlefield. As a smaller community they kept to themselves, often excelling in key areas: the math fair, volunteering and the choir. And it was in the latter that I met my first serious love: Jenny Lui.

I was, alas, reluctantly part of the music class. The terrifying Sister Thibault, one of only two nuns who had survived the turning of our school into a comprehensive high school, forced me to join. One didn't negotiate with Sister T. Although she was only 4' 8", she towered over everyone. If she fixed you with her angry stare, you turned immediately to jelly. You might pee a little in your under-pants too, just to show you were taking her seriously. Even the tough guys from the gym club avoided her if they could. One had even bowed once when he got caught between classes without a hall pass. So, when Sister T. said you were joining the choir, you joined the choir, even knowing it would leave you open to ridicule from the school bullies.

But every cloud has a silver lining, and mine was Jenny Lui, a Chinese girl from what I imagined was a prominent family, who was head of the math and debating clubs. She dressed impeccably and was always beautifully groomed. She had small, perfectly white teeth unencumbered by braces, the other bane of my existence. From the first moment I saw her I knew immediately that she would become my wife. Failing that, I fantasized that I might share a soft drink, or at least sit at a table in the same building with her. The last goal I knew, was truly achievable.

I must be honest. I would not normally have deigned to direct my heart in Jenny's direction. After all, she was a Soprano. In my school, though I'm told this is true in the wider world, Sopranos are a rarified species hovering above the rest. If she had been an Alto, I wouldn't even have hesitated. But it came to pass that the Tenors — which I was generously called, though puberty made me a cross between Michael Jackson and Barry White at times — were stationed near the Sopranos. Or, more to the point, because I was a short kid, I was placed next to Jenny in the front row so that I wouldn't block the view of the other taller — or as Sister T. put it — the more important kids. (I think she meant the other Sopra-nos.)

If the choir was a curse, the decision to do *The Sound of Music* was surely the lowest point of my existence — and goodness knows I'd had plenty of those already. It was expected that we would put together a number of songs for the end-of-year performance, and the grand finale was to be a medley featuring 'Edelweiss' — German for I can't believe you're making me wear these Bavarian shorts in public — through to 'Climb Ev'ry Mountain.' The feature moment, which I couldn't object to, was Jenny's solo on 'Maria.' But it was the insipid 'Do-Re-Mi' that gave me the greatest hope, because in a moment of serendipity that I am grateful for to this day, I was asked to sing the counterpoint with Jenny herself. When she said, 'Doe, a deer, a female deer,' I was the romantic stud bucket that repeated it back a few beats later, as passionately as I could and staring deeply into her eyes — perhaps too deeply. Once or twice hers began to twitch as I glared at her and she lost her place in the song. But that's how love works, I guess.

Choir practice was always held twice a week at lunch, once during music class, and then at least one evening after school. It was after one such late night practice that I found myself, quite by accident, following the same path home as Jenny. The dictionary refers to this as a 'coincidence.' Police reports call it 'stalking.' Be that as it may, I wanted to know where she lived, and I followed at a discrete distance, occasionally accidentally throwing myself into a bush or shrub when she happened to turn around. In the end she reached a dilapidated tailor's shop and disappeared inside.

Mesmerized, I approached the dusty window of the shop, filled with ancient artifacts that I was sure were from the Shang dynasty. Rare and exquisite instruments of torture, designed for medieval purposes that defied modern reasoning, occupied the meager display. One especially sinister implement held centre place in the window. 'What is that?' I must have said it out loud, because the next thing I heard was Jenny's Soprano-perfect voice: 'It's an old sewing machine, idiot.' I couldn't tell what amazed me more. That her Chinese culture had created a sewing machine that looked like a prized weapon from the Spanish Inquisition, or that Jenny had actually spoken to me. On purpose. I wondered if she had broken the Soprano code. Or perhaps it didn't apply outside the choir loft.

'Wow,' I said, as suavely as I could, 'I love antiques.'

'What are you doing here?' she asked, a look of deep suspicion on her exquisite, soloist, face.

'I was just innocently making my way home, minding my own business, and just happened to notice this store. Yours?'

'My dad's. He's a tailor. Doesn't your dad own a shop? Ten blocks from here in the other direction?'

I nodded my head seriously. 'Yes,' I said, excited that she knew of me. 'But I get bored very easily, so I always take a different way home. Keeps him on his toes. He never knows what direction I'll arrive from.'

Jenny stared at me with what looked like — I was going to say desire, but I think it was disgust. 'You're a weird kid,' she said at last. 'Stop staring me down during the song. It's creeping me out.' With that she turned on her heel and disappeared back into the small exotic store. A sign on the door's window, in green neon cursive, read '*nsap*'.

I had no idea what it meant. More mysterious Chinese stuff. And because I didn't want Jenny's father to come out and show me what the sewing machine was really used for, I hurried along, getting hopelessly lost, and eventually finding my way home after dark.

My father was in his store, pricing new stock, and I plopped down next to him. 'I think I'm in love,' I sighed dramatically.

'Again?' he said, with what I thought could have been more compassion.

'No, this time is for real. Jenny Lui. She's beautiful and talented and truly mysterious.'

'Why is she mysterious?' my father asked, flicking the pricing gun rapid-fire on a dozen boxes of rat poison.

'She's a Soprano,' I answered wistfully.

'Can it be cured?' Normally, my father's humour was always welcomed, but clearly he didn't know true love when he saw it. He must have registered my deep existential angst, and he softened immediately. He placed his hand on my shoulder. 'You're covered in leaves. What did you do? Wrestle a tree? You'd better get cleaned up before your mother sees you.'

'Thanks dad,' I said, only half hearing him. 'I knew you'd understand.' And with that I retreated to my room.

The following day was equal parts excitement and terror. I knew I would see Jenny again in music class, and I couldn't wait. I was also terrified of the reception I'd get. I had been subtle in my stalking, but she'd discovered me nonetheless. I couldn't be sure how she'd respond. Come the hour, though, something unexpected happened. As I was making my way to class, I turned the corner and saw Jenny, kneeling on the floor, picking up her scattered schoolbooks. Ronald Turgeon, my mortal enemy, was standing over her making racist comments and screaming at her to go back to her country. Cruelty wasn't unusual for him, and normally everyone steered clear, myself included, but for whatever reason I rushed beside Jenny and started to help her with her books. I looked up at Ronald, and without thinking hissed, 'Not cool, dude. Not cool.'

I'm not sure what I expected would happen, but luckily almost all the kids had fled the hallway, so Ronald didn't have an audience. He picked me up and slammed me into the nearest locker. 'It's cool if I say it's cool,' he scowled, and then, rather surprisingly, walked away. I was aware of my hands shaking uncontrollably as I picked myself up off the ground. By this time, Jenny had collected her books and came over to me.

She pinned me down with her Soprano stare: 'Well that was stupid,' she said. 'He could have beaten the crap out of you.' She started to turn away and then paused. 'Thanks, dork.'

I tried to do a casual salute. 'No problem, little lady,' I stammered, imitating John Wayne.

She looked at me with a combination of disbelief and contempt. 'Don't ruin the moment.' And although she walked away, I was pretty sure she smiled with her eyes, and later in class, as we sang our song, I was equally certain she nodded approvingly. 'Not bad,' she said later, 'You didn't completely suck.' As I'm sure is obvious, I wasn't well equipped to deal with that level of unmitigated flattery, so I just said nothing, which in retrospect, was probably the right thing to do.

A few days later, after the evening choir practice, Jenny invited me to walk her home. 'My dad said he can show you how the old sewing machine works. If you're interested.' I gladly agreed, and we walked the few blocks to her place, not really saying much. She did pause next to a large bush at one stage and said, 'Did you want to jump in here again?'

'No,' I assured her, 'that was a one off.' This time she actually laughed. As we approached the tiny store, I began to rehearse all the cultural stereotypes about China that I had learned from the action movies I loved, wondering what arcane artifacts I would find in the tailor's shop. We got to the door, with its mysterious green slogan — '*nsap*' — and then walked into the dusty silence. After a moment a small man emerged from the back and made his way towards me. He extended his hand and shook mine formally. As I looked around the shop, I saw all the same tell-tale signs of poverty that marked my father's store: the threadbare carpet, the broken cash register, the peeling paint. I turned as the door swung shut behind me and realized that the mysterious writing was facing inward, and I had been reading it back to front. The sign actually said '*open*' in green cursive lettering.

'My daughter tells me you are interested in instruments of death and torture,' he said. 'So let me show you the sewing machine. It has pierced many a finger over the centuries. Later, if you have the stomach for it, we can listen to my daughter play trombone. Truly terrifying.'

Jenny hung her head melodramatically. 'It's going to be a long night. You guys are on your own.'

I never did marry Jenny. Despite my best efforts we only managed a couple of awkward dates, but it was close to the end of the school year, and after the major concert we all went our separate ways. But I would like to think that every time she watches *The Sound of Music,* she thinks of me. *Edelweiss,* my dear Jenny, *Edelweiss.*

Twenty-five

CASINO ROYALE

My parents were poor, though few in the neighbourhood, or even the extended family, knew this. In part it was because my dad owned a struggling store, but in the eyes of the community this made him a business owner. Prior to his marriage to my mother, he was considered quite the catch, and after they wed, she was subjected to years of nastiness by customers whose unwed daughters blamed the 'English woman' for taking a French heartthrob off the market. Over the years, the criticism grew to wear her down, even as she gradually learned, and rather charmingly mangled, the Québécois dialect.

Despite the language barrier, my mother was quite popular with the salesmen and trades people who frequented my father's store, largely because she was charming and laughed easily and honestly at their jokes. She had a refined air, but also looked as though she needed protecting, and this was an intoxicating combination in a space of concrete dust and paint fumes. 'She's a breath of fresh air,' I heard one of the salesmen say as he hacked his way through his two-pack a day habit.

Perhaps because of this unrefined environment, my mother saved her pennies so that we could go out for dinner occasionally, preferably at the local Chinese restaurant where the manager always set the table efficiently, with crisp folded napkins that my mother secretly coveted. I was convinced that the restaurant was a front for a secret gambling den, just like in the movies, which made the place especially appealing. Once when we were there a group of businessmen chose the table next to us, and I watched as they ordered copious amounts of food and alcohol. The lead figure was smooth and poised, with a glistening comb-over that he occasionally patted as he generously disbursed what was clearly a bucketful of witticism. His colleagues, desperate to shine in his eyes, lapped up every word.

I studied his hand gestures, how he flicked the napkin free and tucked it roughly into his collar. He drank his beer from a chunky glass and wrapped his hairy knuckles around it the way I imagined James Bond would hold a martini. And at the end, his eyes sweeping the nervous guests, he announced to the waiter, 'All on one bill!' The chorus of weak protests and genuine gratitude from his underpaid associates rang out and I thought how powerful he seemed. This was what Wall Street must be like, I thought. The only thing that could make the evening better would be if a swordfight broke out and everyone was horrifically wounded. But no outing is perfect.

At our table we safely ordered the butterfly shrimp and the sweet and sour chicken and gratefully watched as the plates, licked clean, were taken away, knowing we wouldn't have to wash up that evening. And my mother's face beamed with pride as my father

paid the bill, pausing to light her cigarette in an equally suave gesture of masculinity. I was grateful to have such concrete role mod-
els to base myself on as I endeavoured to be a man of the world. I
knew that practice made perfect, however, and so carefully saved
my own pocket money so that I could one day invite Marian Keys,
my latest obsession, to dinner.

Marian was a gifted gymnast, and she was partly why I had
joined the school gymnastics team. Mostly it was because all the
toughest school bullies were there and by joining the club it cut by
half the number of people who picked on me daily. But one of the
real perks of being in the club, besides the health benefits, was that
every day the boys were asked to 'spot' the girls when they were
doing their floor routines. This meant, if I was extremely lucky,
that my hand actually made contact with Marian's back as she at-
tempted her backflip. If I was exceedingly fortunate, she might slip
and crash into me. Though it hadn't happened, I imagined the ec-
stasy of lying crumpled on the floor with her in my arms, blood
flowing majestically from my broken nose. One could certainly
dream.

In any event, as the end of term approached, my desperation
made a pact with my bravado, and in the course of a particularly
complex routine I managed to invite Marian out to the local Chinese restaurant. I had studied how this was done, and I felt sure
that I could master the suave sophistication of the Businessman
Bond, flicking my napkin stylishly while lighting Marian's cigarette
… if she happened to take up smoking in the next few days.

It is a complex thing for a man of the world to invite a sophisticated woman out to dinner for the first time, and I was reasonably

sure that I had covered all my bases. 'Do you eat?' I had asked incisively, and in the end I was pretty certain that I had invited her for an early dinner on the upcoming Saturday. I had ensured that I could pay for most things on the menu, but also practiced recommending the more affordable options: 'The sweet and sour fish is especially popular at this time of year. Very little Salmonella. And the Sprite is to be recommended. Very Spritey!' I was ready.

For the rest of the week I made sure to smile at her debonairly in the hallways, knowing that we shared a secret of great intimacy. Even when the local jock rested his hand casually on her shoulder, I knew that he was just a pretender. She had already committed to dinner with me, and I knew from her tenacity on the uneven bars that she did not give up until she'd mastered her routine. She would not give up on me.

Come the fateful day I made sure that I was wearing my cleanest underwear, and I tried to use a ton of hair gel to reproduce the comb-over look of the James Bond Salesman. It wasn't incredibly successful, in part because I had so much hair that it just looked like a particularly dyslexic bird had built a two-story condo on my forehead. But still. It was a look. I also wore my best windbreaker, the one with the inside pocket that would let me whip out my wallet stylishly when she inevitably insisted on sharing the bill.

'I wouldn't hear of it, Moneypenny,' I practiced in the mirror.

'Who's Moneypenny?' my father asked, happening to walk by at that precise moment.

'Only the most seductive woman in the entire school. I am dining with her this evening.'

My father nodded appreciatively. 'That's my boy. A regular Sean Connery. Be back by 7:30.'

As I left the house and walked the three blocks to the restaurant, I tried to convince myself that I didn't have a curfew, *per se*. It was just that my father was keen to hear the news as soon as possible. So by the time I reached the restaurant I was quite positively disposed, though I could feel a bit of the adrenaline and fear running through my limbs. I reached self-consciously into my pocket where I had stashed a pack of mint candy pretend cigarettes and pulled one out. If she happened to be there, her first sight of me would be a roguish one. I capped off the look with a pair of dark sunglasses.

When I entered the restaurant, I managed to walk into a prominent gold lion that guarded the entrance, and then to trip over the ornate carpet. In retrospect, perhaps the glasses were a shade too dark and mysterious. Thankfully, Marian hadn't quite arrived. I made my way to my favourite table, which guaranteed that I would have an unobstructed view of the door, and I proceeded to make myself comfortable. The cranky owner came by and slammed a glass of water in front of me. 'I'm waiting for someone,' I said in the poshest accent I could muster. 'A lady!' He snapped his note pad shut and walked away.

After the first half hour he appeared again, a look of annoyance on his face. I toyed with the idea of flicking the napkin out and laying it across my lap, just to show him I was serious, but I wanted to save the maneuver for Marian. Instead, I looked at him earnestly and said, 'I'll have a spring roll as I wait my good man. And a Sprite. Shaken not stirred.' The owner began to speak, and then thinking better of it, no doubt sensing my worldliness, walked away. Ten seconds later he reappeared, slapped down a spring roll on a miniature plate, and banged the Sprite next to it. I must say that it isn't a great idea to order a canned soda shaken, and despite my best intentions I had to use the napkin to dry my face and clothing after the soft drink exploded generously all over me. As best I could, I made it look as though it was intentional. 'So refreshing,' I might have said. But perhaps not aloud.

After an hour, with me picking at the entrails of my spring roll and draining my glass, I began to suspect that Marian had the wrong address. Mortified, I wondered if I had unintentionally sent her to a different restaurant. I should have offered to pick her up, though I knew her older brother was especially fearsome and didn't really want to risk it on a first date.

The manager, sensing my distress, brought another can of Sprite to the table and placed it down gently. 'Free refill,' he said. 'Sometimes the traffic is bad or lady have trouble finding the place.' It was an unexpected gesture of kindness, and after two hours I realized that my first dinner date was not to be. I was past my curfew. I'd finally finished the spring roll, and I'd emptied the second Sprite and needed the washroom something fierce. It was time to accept defeat and call for the check. I lifted my finger the way the debonair businessman had done, and when the owner came to the table I announced, somberly, 'All on one bill.'

The owner looked at me kindly and smiled. I'd never seen him smile before. He patted me gently on the shoulder. 'It's on the house ... Mr. Bond.'

Twenty-six

SHALOM

I have to be honest. All of the efforts I made to become a ladies' man were a spectacular failure. I knew the advice columns couldn't be wrong because they were written by experts, so it had to be me. But something my father said stuck with me. We were working in the back yard, unpacking a new shipment of garden tools, when I complained about not being interesting enough. I explained that I didn't seem to be attractive to anyone. I told him about the self-help columns I'd read.

He nodded thoughtfully. 'It's like that first guitar I bought you at the thrift shop.' I studied his face and tried to follow. Usually, with my dad, you just had to wait. Eventually it always made sense. 'You thought you couldn't play, but it was just too big for your hand. And when I got you the electric guitar, with the smaller neck, your hand suddenly fit around it, and you could make the chords.' Light was beginning to break through the clouds of incomprehension. 'Those advice columns assume everyone is the same. But we all have a different grip. Focus on yours. Write your own column.'

It was like a light bulb had turned on. I was trying to be a suave and sophisticated playboy, but I was in junior high. It would be a couple of years before I owned my own cars and private jets. In the meantime, though, I could fill in the blanks; build the knowledge I needed to be a man of the world. I knew just what I had to do.

When I returned to school the next day I dropped by the counsellor's office. As soon as Slomo Bundengelder saw me, he panicked and began to scurry towards his office. 'It's okay,' I assured him. 'Your advice worked.' That stopped him in his tracks. I'm sure no one had ever said that to him before. He looked frantically around the room as though checking for hidden cameras. 'I'm following a different path. I actually just want the schedule for the school clubs.' Slomo looked at me as though I was trying to trick him, but I think he saw that I was a different man than the sexually depraved maniac he'd met earlier.

'Clubs?' he asked.

'Yes. Expand my horizon. Try new things. My dad says I need to write a column.'

'Okay,' he said, still unsure. He moved towards a messy desk in the waiting room, watching me all the while as though I might pull out a knife and stab him while he was distracted. 'Clubs?' he repeated, and I nodded. His hand reached into the scattered papers the way someone might reach for a trip wire in an action movie and grabbed a sheet of paper. Nothing exploded. 'Do you mean like this?'

He handed it to me tentatively, as though he was feeding a starving lion and his hand was a sirloin steak. I scanned it. 'Yes, exactly. My father says I should expand my knowledge, so I thought I'd join a few clubs, widen my frame of deference.'

I could tell that Slomo was relieved. 'That's a really great idea. Nothing does more to help us appreciate life than widening our frame of ... *reference*.' For some reason he emphasized the last word.

'I know, that's what I just said. Thank you.' With that I literally skipped out of his office and used the free period I had to scan the clubs and societies' page. My goal was to pick something cultural, something totally new to me, all in the hope of becoming a more well-rounded person. I knew from my intensive reading on the subject that women, for whatever reason, couldn't resist a round person. Luckily, my school was rich in choices. Not in rounded persons but in clubs. There was a cooking club, but that wasn't the roundedness I was after. I skipped over the standard clubs that geeks were normally drawn to — the chess club, the debater's society, the mastication club. I confess I didn't know what that last one was about, but the poster advertising it was disgusting. (Later I realized it was just a poster about the dangers of gum disease, but I wasn't interested either way.) In the end, after careful study, I chose something called the Jewish Hillel Club. I'd never heard of it, but the poster had pictures of faraway lands and a very cool candelabra. I loved candles.

I was lucky that the group met that evening, and that neither the choir nor the gym club had training at that time. It was destiny. I packed my things and went in search of the classroom. When I got there someone had taped a familiar star image to the door. I couldn't quite put my finger on it, but I'd seen it elsewhere and as I was wracking my brain to remember, the cutest girl on the planet approached me and rational thought, such as it was, completely abandoned me.

'I'm Rachel Rosenbaum,' she said and put out her hand. 'Are you here for the movie?'

I shook her hand and fought the now familiar paralysis that crept across my tongue whenever I was approached by a beautiful woman. I thought of my catastrophic first kiss, braces locked for an eternity, and my throat started to constrict. But then I remembered the image on the door and pointed. 'The Star of David?' she asked, no doubt wondering if I was a special needs kid.

'Yes,' I finally managed to say. 'I visited your building once, down the road from here. Is it still there?'

She looked impressed with my worldliness already. 'You mean the Beth Shalom Temple?'

'Yes, the Slalom Temple.'

'Where exactly would it go? It covers two blocks.'

'Quite right,' I said, accidentally and regretfully adopting a British accent. I suddenly remembered the name for the boss man at the temple I'd visited years earlier and threw it in as casually as I could to impress her. 'I recall helping the Ray-Bye with his religious formation.' My nervousness made me mispronounce my words something fierce. She didn't look as impressed as I'd hoped.

'The *Rabbi*,' she repeated, correcting my pronunciation and sounding slightly annoyed, 'is the city's most respected Rabbinic scholar. *You* helped *him*?'

I nodded as wisely as I could. 'It's pronounced differently in Britain,' I mumbled, but I was shuffling backwards towards the smiled sweetly. 'We can just watch TV, right?' I nodded obediently. 'And my aunt just lives next door, for goodness's sake, so if I need anything I can call her. We'll be fine. Don't worry and just have fun.' With that my parents took their leave, my mother looking back uncertainly, as though she was abandoning me to a child trafficking ring.

'Well,' Katherine said once we were alone. 'I hope you're not going to cause me any trouble.' She wriggled out of her jacket to reveal a tight-fitting cardigan. It seemed unnecessarily low-cut for the occasion, but I was definitely not complaining. Most unfortunately, there was a delicate gold crucifix hanging right between her bulging breasts. To say that this caused me some confusion is to understate how profoundly my value system was at war with itself. I was also somewhat annoyed. Until that moment I hadn't much thought about girls. Suddenly, she was all I could think about.

I shook my head the way they do in the cartoons. It seemed to help. 'Not at all! Make yourself at home.'

'Well, that sounds like an excellent idea. Where's your booze?' I hadn't expected that either. She was full of surprises. 'Not beer or crap like that. I mean proper alcohol.'

Neither of my parents drank as such. My dad would have a beer to be polite, my mother a glass of wine. But it wasn't something they did. So there weren't bottles of scotch or gin hidden away in a cupboard which I might clandestinely sip from, adding water to keep the levels right. I'd seen the movies. I knew what kids did. None of this interested me. 'There's some cherry brandy,' I offered lamely. 'My mother uses it to cook.'

Katherine shot me such a disappointed look that I felt guilty. 'It'll have to do,' she said. She fished in her bag and then looked horrified, though it seemed like a poor acting job to me. 'Oh no!'

'What? What happened?'

Katherine looked distraught. Well, she looked like someone who was trying to appear distraught, but who couldn't quite pull it off. Perhaps she didn't much care how authentic it was. And to be honest, when she 'accidentally' pulled at her cardigan in concern and exposed more of her breast than I'd ever seen in real life, I would have given her an Academy Award just for breathing. 'I'm out of cigarettes,' she pouted. 'I can't possibly stay here without my smokes.' She looked at me with sensuous puppy eyes — assuming that puppies could be sensuous of course.

I shrugged helplessly. 'I don't smoke.'

'Your mom?'

'Honestly, she buys it pack by pack. She'd have it with her.'

Katherine made a great show of checking through her change purse. 'You know, I could just run next door to the *Dépanneur* and get some. Except....'

'Except?'

'I seem to be a bit short,' she complained, disappointment heavy in her voice. Her hand, poor thing, was clearly too heavy for her fragile physique to sustain and she hooked her thumb between the buttons, for support of course, and let her arm hang down. The cardigan stretched heroically, unintentionally exposing parts of her prominent bosom. I was worried that her breasts might catch cold.

'I could ... lend you some money,' I said charitably, my voice surprisingly high all of a sudden.

'Really?' I nodded, rather too eagerly I thought. 'I couldn't,' she said, and her poor hand dragged more heavily against her top.

'No! No! I must,' I insisted insistently.

She smiled and waited for me to retrieve my wallet. I pulled out what I thought was the price of a pack of cigarettes. She saw what I was proposing and looked unimpressed. She continued to struggle valiantly to support her arm which seemed to tug more and more against the beleaguered buttons. Gravity was a cruel mistress and it was hard not to admire Katherine's efforts despite her disability. Given the circumstances, I was able to see quite clearly that she wasn't wearing a bra, which was now apparently the fashion. Not that I had had any opportunity to research the matter at any length. But I could see the merits of this type of investigation in the future.

For now, I concentrated on staying hydrated — especially my lips which had become preternaturally dry. Perhaps I was dying I thought briefly, but the speed at which my heart was beating suggested otherwise. That and other physical manifestations made me feel decidedly … alive. I pulled a few more dollars out of my wallet, but her shoulders sagged, and she flashed a rather disappointed moue in my direction. Her poor arm also seemed to get heavier and heavier, accidentally pulling her cardigan down, down, until I finally handed over all my savings. Then she smiled and kissed me on the cheek, pushing up against me rather unnecessarily, but not unpleasantly.

'You're a lifesaver,' she said. 'You're okay here until I get back, right? It's just next door.' I nodded again, feeling the sweat pooling on my lip and forehead. Then she left. She returned a few hours later just as my parents pulled up.

'He was no trouble at all,' she said as my father paid for her services.

After she left my father jokingly told my mother, 'Mustn't do that too often. Can't afford it!'

'You can say that again,' I thought, but strangely, I wasn't bitter in the least.

door. In some discos it was called a moonwalk. I was sure she hadn't noticed. 'Yes, I rendered assistance. He didn't seem to know alot about Jesus's Canadian connection.'

Rachel looked at me like I had a gecko climbing out of my nostril. Then she started to laugh. 'Holy crap you had me going there. I thought you were some imbecilic moronic lunatic.'

'That's a lot of adjectives,' I said.

'Oh man. You were just yanking my chain.'

I started to fake-laugh as well, still, unfortunately, with a British twang. 'You can't take things too seriously, am I right?'

Rachel's smile was rapturous. 'Very right. Well, the film starts in twenty minutes. So go grab some food and then I'll introduce you to some of the other kids.'

'Okay,' I said. 'Right Ho! I just have one other commitment, but I'll be back in a jiffy … *if I can*,' I added, making it seem like I had a packed calendar. I backed away slowly and then as soon as I was clear of the door I bolted. I took the societies sheet with me and headed to the library to research her club. Imagine my shock when I discovered that there was an entirely different religion out there. No wonder the Rabbi hadn't converted when I explained how Catholicism worked. He just needed more time. It was a lot to unpack. And, to be fair, so did I. As difficult as it was to admit, I had to approach matters — including matters of the heart — at a slower pace and in my own way. I realized that it was pointless to rush it.

Needless to say, I didn't make it back in time for the film, though I did see Rachel once or twice after that at school events. In fact, once as I walked by, I saw her point my way and I overheard her tell her group of friends: 'That guy ... funniest kid in the school. British I think.'

So perhaps I was becoming a man of the world after all.

Twenty-seven

DON JUAN

Although I was obsessed with women, I classified myself as more of an old-school romantic — which admittedly for me meant a junior-high-school romantic. How I interpreted this, via Byron, Leonard Cohen's *Death of a Ladies' Man*, *The Hardy Boys* and *Zen and the Art of Motorcycle Maintenance*, was that God had put me on this earth to lighten women's burdens. It is true that I wasn't entirely sure what those burdens were, but I was ready to share the load should I be needed, and that meant that I had to make myself available when called upon. Though first, I knew, I had to be called upon. Which admittedly wasn't happening much.

I had tried different tactics in my frantic school years: a pointless meeting with the school counsellor, a book on hypnosis that kept putting me to sleep, and even a box of magic tricks meant to catch someone's eye. My attempt to make a card appear from my sleeve had unfortunately backfired, and I had almost taken Julie LaRoche's eye out when the card, primed on an over-tightened rubber band, had flicked from my sleeve to her face. She lessened her own burden by giving me a bloody nose in return, so I felt that universal balance had been restored. Somehow, though, there had to be more.

I didn't totally understand the books I insisted on reading well before my time, but I got the gist of some of them. Forcing myself through Lord Byron's *Don Juan*, for example, I understood that, like his hero, I wasn't a womanizer, but rather a man too easily seduced by a woman's charms. Assuming, that is, that a woman — any woman — paid the least bit of attention to me.

It was the final year of junior high, and a prom was rumoured to be happening, and I suppose everyone was preternaturally aware of the need to have a partner for the big night. Karl, who was quite practical, speculated that most girls would go out with a guppy if it meant they weren't alone on Prom night, and since the male to female ratio at our school desperately favoured men, my friend was quite sure that we might be lucky guppies after all.

His theory, while not exactly flattering, proved to be correct, though unfortunately I missed the signs entirely. A number of girls who would not have given me the time of day, suddenly dropped hints around me — subtle, but one would have thought unmistakable. Lisa Giannonnie, for example, asked if I was planning on taking anyone to the prom and if so who would it be and would it likely be an Italian girl, and 'By the way I'm Italian.' I did my best to read between the lines but couldn't guess who she had in mind.

Her friend Anna Maria Bouscella similarly began to drop subtle hints. 'You don't want to be the only shithead not to have a date,' she suggested coyly one afternoon after Biology. 'No,' I answered honestly. 'That would really suck.' She looked genuinely confused when I walked away. It was a pity, too, because both Lisa and Anna

Maria were lovely. I would have given my right arm to go out with either one of them. If only they were remotely interested in me.

I caught up with Karl in the cafeteria, and we compared notes. It's important to understand that he was taller, stronger and ten times better looking than I was. He had the sort of Germanic good looks that caused girls to giggle, literally, when he spoke to them. He had blond hair and a square jaw like you see in the cartoons. He was also fixated on bodybuilding, so he barely noticed any of this attention, obsessed instead on flexing at inappropriate times. You could be speaking with him about a matter of life and death — an outbreak of acne for example — and you would catch him checking his reflection in a nearby mirror instead of concentrating on the tragedy at hand. In the cafeteria, though, surrounded by food, he was able to focus, and we compared notes and agreed that despite the rumours, girls just weren't interested in us and that was that.

Karl was German, he kept reminding me, so he was pragmatic. 'I'll just wait till the week before prom and see who isn't taken.' For me this was an outrage. Prom was just a commodity, a social construction, an artifice. But the girl you brought with you mattered. It had to be an affair of the heart or best not to go at all. I tried to explain this to Karl, described how I had almost lost a testicle to love once, but that the hope alone had been worth it. It was no use. 'I have to go do my reps,' he announced, and polished off his sandwich in two bites.

After he left, one of my classmates sat down in his place. Cathy Varsie had always been nice to me, and I suspect, in retrospect, that she may even have had a crush on me. She could tell by my expression that I was wounded deep in my soul. 'Are you constipated?' she asked, and the concern in her voice was palpable.

'No, Cathy, I'm not constipated. I am troubled deep in my soul.'

'Fair enough. Got a date for the prom yet?'

It was all too much. 'Why does everyone keep asking me that?' I exclaimed. 'We can't all be Hugh Heffner.' And with that I stormed from the cafeteria. Honestly, it was one thing to be unwanted, but quite another to be reminded of it at every turn. There was only one thing I could do. I went back to the Library and checked out the book on hypnosis. Needless to say it didn't help, but I had a restful weekend.

Come Monday I was quite beside myself. There were only five short months until Prom night, and I didn't have a prospect in mind. And so, I decided to take Karl's advice to heart. I would wait for the desperate crumbs to fall my way in the waning hours — minutes perhaps — before Prom night. It wasn't sure-fire, but at least I could concentrate on more pressing matters in the interim.

That was when Sandra Mohammed walked into my life. Quite literally. Tall like a long cool drink of water, with raven flaxen hair that flowed like a cascade of water over Niagara Falls, and poised like a gazelle about to take flight at the first sight of a hungry lion — and yes I'd read my first romance novel over the weekend — Sandra slammed into the door of my open locker knocking both of us to the ground. We sat there stunned like … well like two people who had just banged their heads together and fallen down. I helped her up.

'Sorry,' I said, fumbling to gather my thoughts. 'I didn't mean to put the door of my locker there. Really careless of me.'

She was rubbing her head. 'S'okay. Totally my fault. I was reading the classroom numbers and just didn't see you.'

'Will you live?' I was debonair and suave enough to ask? 'How many fingers do I have?'

'Ten I hope?' she answered, and then panicking momentarily, 'Not that you *have* to have ten fingers.' She paused uncertainly. '*Do* you have ten fingers?'

'Technically eight and a couple of thumbs, though my mother says I'm all thumbs.'

She looked relieved. 'Okay. As long as you don't think I was being judgmental about anything. If you have a disability that's totally cool with me.'

I wasn't sure what she'd heard about me, but I sure wasn't planning on volunteering any compromising information. 'No! I'm a hundred and ten percent undisabled,' I reassured.

'Well, your math isn't great, but okay.'

As the tinny echo of the locker concussion began to fade, we shared a bit more about ourselves. She had just transferred to our school, leaving friends behind, and was keen to get to know her new environment. 'Leave it to me,' I assured her. 'I know all about this place. Practically born here.'

'So math and genealogy are your weak points,' she said, laughing, and then grabbed my hand. My actual hand! The one with all ten fingers. Well, distributed normally across my other body part. 'So lead the way, hombre. Let's see what this puppy has to offer.'

'You mean the school, right? The puppy reference, I mean, that's a simile?'

'Metaphor. But yes, I mean the school. Show me all the sights.'

I felt empowered, except grammatically. 'Okay then. Come this way. Let me show you the gym. If all goes well, this is where we'll have the end of year Prom. You going with anyone? 'Cause if you don't know anyone, I'd be happy to oblige.'

'Sure,' she said. 'But I want a corsage.'

'I, I don't drive,' I said.

She smiled then. 'You're funny. Okay, show me this den of future iniquity.'

And that was how I went from being a guppy to a barracuda.

Twenty-eight

DIRTY DANCING

When Mrs. Deiter, the gym teacher's wife, announced that she was starting a dance class to help us prepare for the Prom, she ascended to the status of sainthood. Unfortunately, none of us could be seen to attend. Our reputations as tough, albeit athletic, hooligans were on the line. We could see what our opponents would do with the fact that we were learning to waltz. It was a dilemma of monumental proportions. We simply couldn't attend, and that was that. Until a rumour began to circulate that the class would be filled with girls. Dozens and dozens of young ladies without partners.

That certainly changed things in my mind. In what I imagined was a truly noble way, I resolved to sneak down to the gym when none of my friends were looking, and dance with as many of the girls as duty required. They would be so grateful.

To do this I would need to head down the hall to the music rooms, backtrack through the garage and auto shop during the class changeover, and then sneak back into the gym through the back door. Which I did. Unfortunately, so did forty-three other boys. What made everything especially unfortunate was that not a single girl turned up. They'd heard that no boys would be there, and so they stayed away.

As everyone knows, when the darkest moment of humiliation has struck, there is always a further fall awaiting. It is a rule of childhood, and a truth of teenage life. Just as we were turning away, shamefaced that we'd been seen by so many, but confident too that no one would speak of this because we were all in it together, we heard the deafening click of the gym door lock. Mrs. Deiter barred the way out and announced that we would be proceeding with the dance lessons anyway. 'Pique a partner, boyes, und ve vill proceed.'

Every humiliating episode of my life flashed before my eyes in that moment. Before I'd discovered the gymnastics club, my father had enrolled me in a judo class so that I could learn to fend off the bullies that seemed to dog my life. As a French kid, forced to attend English school by a well-meaning father, I was victimised by the English boys who saw me as the enemy, and then by the French who called me a traitor. As the smallest kid in school, I was the perfect candidate to be made an example of – and Judo would put a stop to this. I pictured myself as a black belt flipping enemies away in all directions.

In reality I walked into the foul-smelling Judo hall only to be paired up with the only girl because we were the same size. It was one of the lowest points of my young life, driven all that much lower when she threw me effortlessly across the room. This wasn't helped by my first words to her. 'I'll be gentle', I'd said, and then I saw the gym blur past at an alarming velocity. My one and only

Judo lesson ended with me storming past my father at the end of the session when he came to pick me up.

'How was it?' he asked hopefully, but I couldn't speak. What was worse? I wondered. Being beaten up by worthy foes, day after day, or being hurled across a room by a girl my own age.

I felt Mrs. Deiter's hands on my shoulders as she directed me towards Ronald Turgeon. He was six foot already, and he kept saying that he hadn't finished growing. I believed him. In fact, he seemed to be growing before my very eyes. Mrs. Deiter cleared her throat. 'Some of you weel 'av to dance the girls' part to start.' I looked up at Ronald – who now stood thirty feet above me. 'Okay I'll lead', I said as casually as I could manage. I felt his fist catapult me across the room. The next thing I knew I was dancing backwards with a bloody nose.

Twenty-nine

THE DAY THE MUSIC DIED

Excitement was building at the prospect of our junior prom. Our school, perhaps because of how rough it was and how huge the student population, was not inclined to encourage parties of any kind. It had been burnt too often. Metaphorically for the most part, though there was at least one small blaze in an auxiliary music room. So giving the green light to a prom, and a junior one at that, seemed both insane and marvelous at the same time. What began as guarded interest quickly built to a frenzy as students realized the school administration was serious and that this might actually go ahead.

I would have been terrified at the prospect if I hadn't accidentally secured a date for the prom. I had a verbal agreement from Sarah Mohammed, the hottest girl who had a locker immediately adjacent to mine. That she had held my hand on our very first encounter and readily accepted my invitation to be my date had certainly raised a few red flags for me about her judgement — but beggars, as my friend Karl constantly reminded me, had few responsibilities so 'who cares what you do?'

I don't think of myself as an especially negative individual, but when it came to women luck was certainly not on my side. My first viable crush, who purposefully sat on the swings with me and even bought me a soda, lost her spleen in a freak accident a week later and pulled out of school. Jenny Lui, the school's most remarkable soprano, had expressed interest, but then school had ended for the summer and her parents moved the family to Vancouver. I had had some catastrophic experiences kissing with braces that had left me scarred for life — not to mention collateral damage on Marie-France Delormier's remarkable, but no longer perfect, lips.

So you'll forgive me if I approached my relationship with Sarah with an incredible, newfound trepidation. Not wanting to risk her death, deportation or facial mutilation, I subtly avoided her every time I saw her. If she happened to round the corner and I noticed in time, I would leap heroically into a nearby broom closet for her protection. I made sure never to be at my locker when she was around — which meant effectively that I basically carried all my things in my backpack all the time.

Once, in a moment of inattention, she snuck up on me in the line-up at the cafeteria. 'Here you are!' she said pleasantly, and I secretly screamed inside. She was tempting fate. Instead of responding, and certain that something fatal might happen to her if we spoke, I doubled over dramatically and clutched my tummy. 'Oh, stomach ache. Gotta go!' And I rushed from the dining hall. I wasn't sure how this was going to work exactly. Prom night was several months away. I couldn't avoid her until then and ensure that she'd still be my date. Wanting a girlfriend and insisting on keeping her alive were essential but somehow mutually exclusive goals.

In the meantime, a minor crisis was emerging over the venue for the big night. School authorities had agreed we could use the huge double gym for the Prom, but a very vocal group of kids were arguing for a fancier place — a nearby hotel that had a ballroom with an actual chandelier. The cost would escalate significantly, and many complained that it would price us out of the event. The kids who led the push for the fancier venue were adamant that nothing short of the hotel ballroom would be suitable. I'd heard through the grapevine that one incentive for this plan was that it had a myriad of ill-lit corridors branching out from the ballroom that would bedevil the most diligent chaperones. Viewed through that lens, it was difficult to argue with their logic.

In the end, the school caved, and the venue was locked in, and a hefty deposit paid. My small group of friends went to work to earn enough to pay for our tickets — and for our dates if we had one. I took an extra shift on the weekend at the local grocery store. Things were looking up as long as my prom date lived to tell the tale. It really was touch and go.

I suppose it was unrealistic for me to imagine I'd avoid Sarah indefinitely, and sure enough one day after school she pinned me down on the bus. I had made the mistake of sitting in a back corner that did not have an escape hatch, and I was busy reading — I want to say Shakespeare, but it was probably a Spiderman comic — and then poof! There she was. My mouth opened to say something, but she was ready for me: 'So help me if you fake an injury right now, I'll break your arm.' Well, that concentrated the mind.

'Sarah,' I started, and then let out a sigh. 'You don't understand. It's for your own protection.'

Her face darkened suddenly and a look of surprising anger transformed her normally radiant face. 'Oh, it all makes sense!' she said, 'that bastard!' I tried to think which one she was referring to: Fate? Cosmic forces writ large? The school mascot? 'Look,' she said, grabbing my hand, 'my older brother always sticks his nose into my business, but you mustn't let him intimidate you. I know he's six foot three, and I know he's a boxer, but really, he's just over-protective. It's so unlikely that he'd actually kill you. And you don't have to worry about me. He's totally afraid of me.'

I must confess that I wasn't sure how to respond. I was both turned on and mortally afraid at the same time. She was, after all, holding my hand on purpose, and not because she was being forced to shake it in a business meeting. That was hot. Yet she had a brother who sounded like a version of the Hulk. I was reading the wrong comic book. 'But your safety is all that matters,' I croaked. Sarah smiled and, completely unexpectedly, kissed me on the lips. Right then and there. Just a quick peck, but truly, without my braces it was a completely different experience. My last kiss had resulted in my lips being pulled through the wire braces, like meat through a grinder. This was even more amazing. Silky soft. Like kissing a pillow … which I may or may not have practiced on in the past. I would like to say that I received the kiss suavely and that I didn't blush a deep shade of red, but that would be a complete lie.

'No more avoiding me,' she whispered. Then she stood and rang the bell.

'Is this your stop?'

'No, I live in completely the other direction. But you're a hard man to track down.' With that she was gone into the night, her dark flaxen hair waving in a turbulent breeze, her hazel eyes reflecting starlight … etc., etc. I was living the dream.

What followed was a deeply uncomfortable but also extraordinary courtship. Despite the pamphlets I'd read on sexually transmissible diseases, a *Playboy* guide to the world's best pick-up lines to be delivered from a pick-up truck, and a brief talk about sex from an older cousin — 'it's fun' — I really didn't have a clue about how one conducted a relationship. Sarah, for all her initial bravado, turned out to be equally timid, so we spent a great deal of time walking with our hands almost touching, with some deeply awkward sessions where we sat within inches of each other but didn't know what to say. Although we didn't kiss again, nor hold hands, it remains one of the most amazing times of my life. When I thought about it carefully, I was one hundred percent certain that I was in love. I just didn't know what to do about it.

Karl, busy flexing in the bathroom mirror, was surprisingly understanding. 'Dude, the more you worry about it the less it will make sense. Basically, on Prom night, you will be forced to dance together, and everything will sort itself out. Like magic.' He was one of the smartest kids in the school, but I had never thought him wise until that moment.

'Thanks man. I appreciate it.'

Later that afternoon, the principal got on the intercom and announced that because none of the original kids who chose the fancy venue had bought tickets, and since so many kids had opted out because of the price, the Prom had to be cancelled. Moreover, because they lost the booking deposit, they wouldn't be able to put on a more modest dance at the school. The Junior Prom was officially called off.

I made my way to my locker and found Sarah there. She was putting away her books. We turned to face each other.

'Well,' I said.

'Well,' she answered.

'Sorry we can't go to the Prom together.'

'Yeah. That's too bad.'

I stood there awkwardly. My inside voice was telling me to invite her to dinner instead. A concert. The opening of a paper bag for goodness sake. Anything. The look on her face told me that she wanted me to ask. But the words wouldn't come. I felt completely paralyzed. 'Well,' I said at last, 'see you.' I turned laboriously and walked away, my heart breaking. I could feel her eyes on me. I realized too late that the exit was in the opposite direction, so I had to sit alone in the Library until I thought enough time had passed. It was late on a Friday afternoon and the place was deserted. The Librarian looked over at me with annoyance. 'We'll be closing in five minutes,' she said curtly.

I thought of Don McLean's hit song 'American Pie.' It was composed in honour of Buddy Holly's untimely death, but as the words ran through my head, I knew it was also written to mark the death of my love life. 'Something touched me deep inside,' I thought melodramatically, remembering the lyrics and the cancelled Prom, 'the day the music died.'

Thirty

THE SQUAWK BOX

At about the same time that the prom was cancelled, the school newspaper, *The Oppressed Learners Club* (I admit that wasn't its real name) was shut down by the Vice-Principal. I may or may not have contributed a critical article about the outrageously heartless decision to cancel the prom without an alternative, and also a few other minor odds and ends about oppressive administrators. Tame, tame stuff. But dictators don't take kindly to criticism, apparently, so we were cancelled. I was sure they would have sent us all to gulags … if we'd had them.

I remember the huge weight of injustice that I carried home with me that evening. It was a wonder I could walk at all. When I got home my father was watching one of the classic movies he adored. Even though his English was improving it was still difficult for him to follow. If there were accents involved, especially British ones, then it was hopeless. But the American movies were accessible, and he had an encyclopedic memory for all the actors. This evening he was watching *Citizen Kane*. It was in Black and White, so I knew it had to be a B-grade, low-budget, arthouse film. I was impressed that my father was giving amateurs a chance.

Despite the complex plot, not helped by us disappearing every ten minutes or so to serve customers, I came away understanding that it was my destiny to become a newspaper baron. (I wanted to set my sights low to ensure success.) And so, in between intense acting by someone with the implausible name of Orson Welles, together with close-ups of snow globes and whatnot, I managed to convince my dad to let me use his famed Gestetner. I had already proven it could be done, admittedly with mixed results, but I was older now and wiser.

I decided that I would produce an underground version of the school paper. It would be called *The Squawk Box*, named after the annoying intercom that the Vice-Principal used each day to read us the riot act. *The Squawk Box* would be unfettered by 'The Man's' dictatorial hand; it would be a voice for the downtrodden, the oppressed, the misunderstood — in other words, the junior high students.

I spent the evening sketching out a logo which I grandiosely referred to as our masthead. I wasn't sure who 'our' was yet, since I was the only one involved, but I was a man of the world, and I knew that all empires started with a humble vision. In truth, though, I was Sir Edmund Hilary tackling the Mount Everest of censorship, and I couldn't let the fear of frostbite and altitude sickness scare me from speaking Truth to Power. It would be true to say that, even before I'd written a single word of our new protest document, I had already prepared my Nobel Prize acceptance speech. Important to note — it would be the first time in the Academy's history that the prize was jointly awarded for Peace and Literature.

The magnitude of my fictional accomplishment initially affected my ability to write, though once I'd identified the key topics of my moral crusade, the ideas flowed. I wrote a dramatic and heart-rending account of the crushed dreams of the junior high students, devastated by the insensitivity of the mandarins that ran the school. It was a sequel to the piece that had shut the paper down. I called it: 'No prom, no Problem? We think not!' I exposed the callousness of the cafeteria staff who limited students to a single paper napkin, even when they served messy tacos. Who did that? And while I was at it, I may have pontificated on the intrusive impact of the intercom during class time. I had actual reports of students flicking their pens in terror when the intercom blared on unannounced. Someone could easily lose an eye.

I confess I was on a roll and may have strayed slightly too far in my unmitigated condemnation of the school. To counter this, I added a feel-good piece about how grateful students were that the school persisted in providing desks for everyone. Of course, there was no plan afoot to remove them, but I was hard-pressed to find something good to say. (I was also surprised to later discover that the powers that be interpreted that particular piece of altruistic writing as sarcasm. Some people can't take a compliment when it's thrust at them.) I debated doing a catchy 'focus' piece on Sister Anne, but time was against me, so I diligently typed up my articles on a stencil and then proceeded to print a few hundred copies double-sided.

The result, I will admit, was not pretty — but by golly it had Pulitzer Prize written all over it — mostly because I'd added those words to the masthead. In retrospect it may have been over-reach, but at the time, it seemed quite likely.

Writing the masterpiece was one thing, distributing it quite another. Without a strong network I had to find an effective mechanism to get the news into the right hands. Luckily, I had anticipated this problem, seeing as I was steps away from being a newspaper baron. I had added an inset piece at the bottom of the second page that shamelessly promoted the up-coming gymnastics competition. I may have used words like: 'Come to support the best-looking, fittest, hottest and most talented students in the school.' Well, in point of fact, those were exactly the words I used. As a result, the entire gymnastics club — male and female — made it their mission to distribute the newsletter to everyone.

I have to be honest; it was an amazing feeling to walk down the corridor and see my classmates reading my searing investigative journalism, and even to witness one or two teachers hiding the newsletter as I passed by, but with a glint of respect for my bravery in their weary eyes. There was a buzz in the air. Followed by a crackling of the eponymous squawk box. I had just taken my place in my Canadian lit. class, and was unpacking my books, when the Vice-Principal's voice summoned me to the main office. In a sign of spontaneous solidarity from my fellow oppressed, the entire class broke out in a breathy: 'Oooooooooooo'se in trouble now?'

I repacked my bag as slowly as I could and then heroically, morosely and somewhat tragically, shuffled my way to the administrative offices. As I stood in the waiting room looking morosely and tragically heroic, I saw virtually the entire staff reading my master-piece, some of them chuckling openly, but when the VP's door opened, they hid their copies hastily. As he always did, the Vice-Principal pointed at me with his crooked, wart-filled finger. (Since becoming a newspaper reporter, I allowed myself a bit of creative license.) 'You. My office. Now.' I wasn't sure why he always spoke in staccato sentences, but I was grateful, as I walked into his room, that I had decided not to write the limerick about his melodious voice as I'd originally planned. *That* would have been sarcasm.

In any event, I took my seat in the over-sized chair and watched as he stomped his way to his desk. 'This unacceptable gar-bage,' he started to say, but then the phone rang. 'You. Sit.' I looked around to make sure that I was, indeed, seated. One never knew. He picked up the phone. 'Ravelli. What? When?' No, no. I'm on my way.' He put down the receiver and stared at it. 'You. Go.' I looked around the room again, not sure if I'd heard right. 'Go!' he shouted, and I gathered my things. When I opened the door of his office the staff jumped back, as though they had all gathered at the door to hear. 'I'll book you a follow-up time,' someone said hastily.

I made my way back to class and everyone acted as though I'd never left. At the very end, after the bell had gone, Maria **Vianetti sidled up beside me. 'What happened? You weren't gone long.'**

I shrugged. 'I got in there and then he told me to leave. The phone rang though. Maybe it was the Pulitzer Prize committee. They read my stuff. Told him to back off?'

Maria looked at me as though she had stepped in dog effluent. 'Seriously? That's what you've got for me? Unbelievable.' And she walked away.

'What?' I shouted after her. 'Could happen.' You never know, I thought.

A few days later we learned that the VP's family had been in a crash while visiting Yellowstone. He'd left the country to take care of things and wouldn't be back anytime soon. I asked Karl if I should do a story about it in the second print run of *The Squawk Box*. 'Dude. You dodged a bullet. Be smart for once. Call it quits.'

PART FOUR

In which our hero is tragically brought down to earth

Thirty-one

ALTER EGOS

I always felt bad for Bullseye and Batman. Unlike virtually every other hero, they didn't actually have superpowers. One was a deadly shot, the other an inventive detective with more toys than Inspector Gadget. But nothing superhuman. Other things bugged me about them as well. Bullseye fired hundreds of arrows, but he never seemed to collect them afterwards. Did he not care about the environment? What if a child stumbled across them and got hurt? The only thing he was super about was littering. Batman, perhaps because he wasn't actually a superhero, was always cranky. It would also be exhausting if you had to speak in that preternaturally gravelly voice all the time. But he did have a cool car.

I preferred my superheroes super heroic-y. But not like Superman. He was annoying for the opposite reason. He was too powerful. The writers had to go to elaborate lengths to make him vulnerable. Otherwise, the comics would last for two pages. The bad guy would come in, fire 8000 rounds of heavy artillery which would bounce off the conveniently bulletproof fabric of his costume, and then Superman would squash the guy. Luckily for the bad guys there always seemed to be a ready supply of Kryptonite on hand. Walmart must have made a killing. I knew that Superman was co-created by a Canadian, so I felt some loyalty towards him, but boy did he make it hard.

Alter egos were another of my pet peeves? Despite working in precise geographical locations no one ever seemed to figure out who was who. Batman at least wore a mask so you could pretend there was a stark difference between him and Bruce Wayne. Superman, though, put on a pair of glasses and all of a sudden, presto-chango, he was unrecognizable! My friend Karl was furious when I said this. 'It's completely believable!' he screamed at me once in front of a group of classmates. So when he put his reading glasses on I made a huge show of acting like I didn't know who he was. 'Guys! Where'd Karl go? Karl! Karl come back! Please. All is forgiven.' He didn't speak to me for a week after that.

For most of my friends, Spiderman was the hero to be. Here was a fellow student, as awkward with girls as most of us, picked on by bullies and lost in the world. His newfound powers were a blessing and a curse, and I'm pretty sure he suffered from acne as well. Since we occasionally went on school excursions, we all could see the possibility that we might one day acquire his power. God knows there were spiders everywhere and the chance that we, too, might be bitten and transformed by a radioactive arachnid was an ever-present possibility. Hope in the midst of the nihilism of algebra.

Despite my encyclopedic knowledge of comics, I was surprised when I discovered that many people actually did have alter egos in real life — an identity different to the one the community knew about. Sometimes the discovery was surprising but heart-breaking. Working in the grocery store one Saturday I ran into Ms. Melville, who had abandoned our English class before it could even get started. She was standing behind a stack of toilet paper and seemed incredibly uncomfortable to see me. When I moved to stand near her, she shifted in the opposite direction, as though she wanted the wall of three-ply to remain between us.

'I was surprised when you left class, Miss,' I started to say, and then she stumbled free of her barrier. I gasped when I saw her over-sized stomach. Her hands moved protectively to cover her tummy. Her face, embarrassed at first, suddenly grew pinched and angry.

'The school doesn't take too kindly to unwed mothers now, does it?'

'Well, we missed you in class,' I added untruthfully.

Her features softened. She looked as though she was going to cry. 'Thank you for saying that,' she whispered, and then started to leave. She paused and turned back towards me, her hand resting on her stomach. 'I read that *Moby Dick* book,' she said. 'Mind-numbingly boring.' I nodded, not sure what to say. 'Don't tell any-one you saw me, okay? I don't really want the kids to know my business.'

I smiled as kindly as I could. 'Of course. I won't say a word.'

A few weeks later my mother's best friend visited the house. Mrs. A. as she was known to everyone, was decades older than my mum. In her youth my mother had been her governess, actually travelling to the US to answer a job ad, an incredibly brave thing to do back then, especially for a young woman. As always happened, the family loved her so much that she became more of a favoured daughter. They actually hired a housekeeper one time to do my mother's job so that they could take her with them on vacation. Years later, Mrs. A. lost her entire family, though I never knew how, and she moved to Canada to be near my mother. I didn't know much about Mrs. A., but she was incredibly kind, and the only woman I knew who had a tattoo. I'd seen it once, when her sleeve caught on the handle of the China cabinet as she was helping me to set the table.

Later that evening, after Mrs. A. had left, I mentioned the tattoo to my mother. 'Pretty cool for a girl to have one,' I said, and my mother stiffened. She wiped her hands on her apron and seemed visibly upset. 'Mom?'

She reached out her hand and I moved over to take it. 'I don't want you to ever say anything about that to anyone. Especially not to Mrs. A., okay?' I nodded, but I didn't understand. 'Mrs. A. was a prisoner in Auschwitz. I want you to look it up, all right? To understand. She's a survivor.' She had such a desperate look in her eyes that I felt frightened. 'She saved my life when I was younger. I was going through a tough time, and she was there for me. When you look at her you should see a hero, understand?'

'Yes,' I said, my heart beating quickly. She was still holding my hand and didn't realize how hard she was squeezing it. 'I understand,' I repeated somewhat desperately, and she smiled, lost in thought, and left the room. When I returned to school after the long weekend, I made a point of visiting the library during my free period and read about the concentration camps. I felt suddenly ashamed about my ignorance, and deliberately gave the Hillel Club a wide berth, too embarrassed to be seen by Rachel Rosenbaum.

Needless to say, when Mrs. A. visited again a few weeks later, I felt awkward around her. I was inordinately aware of her covered wrist and went to ridiculous extremes to avoid looking at it. When the meal was over, and my mother left the room to make the tea, I had no choice but to make conversation. 'My mother says you saved her life,' I blurted into the uncomfortable silence and to my surprise Mrs. A. chuckled.

'She may say that,' she whispered, as though sharing a deep secret, 'but your mother saved mine.'

'She says you're a hero.'

'Oh my! Well, the same is true about her.'

I wanted to ask more, but my mother called out to me and I left to help. Later in the evening I found them sitting in our miniscule living room. They were holding hands. Neither was talking. They were just sitting in the near darkness, each with a sad smile on her face. I realized that night that heroes came in different shapes and sizes, and that origin stories weren't as simple as they seemed in the comics. I had stumbled on their alter egos without quite understanding what I'd discovered. When I asked my dad about it, he answered, cryptically, 'when it's appropriate for you to know, you'll know.' Usually, he circled back and made things clear, but this time he just smiled sadly. 'All in good time,' he said. 'All in good time.'

Thirty-two

BLACK AND WHITE (AND RED ALL OVER)

The world was getting increasingly complex. It had always been difficult, but in a sense, for me at least, everything had always been black and white. There were good guys and bad guys. My parents were happy, or they were sad. If the latter, I could goof around until they felt better, and all was right with the world. On the alien planet designed to conduct horrific experiments on young minds (aka high school), there had been nice teachers and mean ones. It was easy to identify the dangerous lifeforms, if not always simple to avoid them. But at least you knew who was who. Then, suddenly, everything seemed to change. A good person could also be another; a blessing could also be a curse. I learned that joy could be authentic and yet sit only precariously above a wounded space that couldn't, wouldn't, ever heal. A space between.

As I approached the waning days of junior high, I discovered the word 'nuance', and there was nothing good about it. In debating club, which I had only briefly tried, we were taught to argue for something and then asked immediately to switch to the opposite view. 'Training your mind to be nimble,' Ms. Joy had said. Now I could see that this was false. There wasn't just right or wrong. There was kind-of-okay, sort-of-bad. There wasn't just evil by day and good by night. The same forces lived inside the one, a Jekyll and Hyde situation where the status quo seemed to be the space of transformation. We were always on the way to something: never just one thing or another — and I mourned the delusional stability I had once known.

Mr. Squalo was one of these chameleons, though I didn't know it at the time. He was the breath of fresh air who appeared in the brutal twilight hours and replaced the sour Vice-Principal who had been the bane of my existence. In contrast to the always-angry VP who clearly hated students and blamed us for ruining what would otherwise be a great job, Mr. Squalo appeared with gusto and humour, genuinely interested in what we had to say.

I had initially been sent to the crusty Vice-Principal's office to discuss an infraction he felt I had committed, only to be met by his replacement who thought my approach was innovative.

'Wait,' he said to me, 'You created a student newsletter on your dad's Gestetner because the principal stopped funding the school paper?' I gave a quick nod, not sure if I should confess outright or wait for him to read me my rights. I watched television. I knew how entrapment worked. 'That's awesome. So why are you here? Am I supposed to give you an award or something?'

'Cash prize,' I blurted and Squalo started to laugh. 'Actually,' I confessed, 'my editorial was ... critical ... of management for defunding the paper. I also wrote a cranky article about how the school cancelled our prom and "they" didn't like it.' I thought I was especially clever because I used air quotes when I said 'they'. I figured I was sufficiently ambiguous so that my lawyers could argue, should things go bad, that I was referring to another, perhaps a splinter revolutionary group, in another high school. To be honest, I began to get lost in my back story, but it turns out it was all for nothing.

'That's insane!' Squalo said. 'Dude, you were doing the right thing.' No one since Mr. McCool had called me dude, well not in a positive way, and I began to let my defenses down. 'You understand, because I'm so new here, I can't really criticize the principal and the executive team. But you know what, I can certainly make a case for how important it is that our students speak up.' He paused as though he'd just heard what he said. 'It won't be popular, but at the very least you shouldn't be here to be disciplined. I have something else in mind.' He put his hand on my shoulder. 'I got your back, okay?' Then he actually hugged me.

Later, in the locker room before gym, I cornered Karl. 'This guy is the real deal.'

'No detention?'

'On the contrary. He practically called me a human rights champion. I think we finally have an administrator who cares what the kids think. He asked me to help him out with some office jobs. Do you want to come with?'

'Hell ya,' Karl said, 'if only to prove that it's impossible for those guys to be good.'

I had arranged to meet Mr. Squalo after school on Wednesday but when I turned up with Karl he seemed a bit put out. 'Oh! Who are you?'

'This is my best mate, Karl. We're in the gym club together. I told him you were a cool guy.'

Mr. Squalo hesitated for a moment and then his face brightened. 'You know what? Many hands make light work. We'll get through the filing all that much faster.' He held his hand out and Karl shook it uncertainly. He pulled him in for a hug. 'Come on in guys and I'll explain the task at hand.'

As we followed him in Karl whispered, 'Check my back. Did he stab me or something?'

'Relax, the guy is cool.'

We spent a half hour helping the new VP move non-essential files from a crowded filing cabinet into labelled boxes, making space for 'new priorities', whatever that was. Afterwards, sweaty and tired, Mr. Squalo pulled out a cooler and handed us a soft drink. 'I really appreciate your help with this.' Then he gave us each ten dollars. We were in shock. 'I believe in fair pay for honest labour. You guys helped me out. And there's more to do. So if you guys are free, let me know.'

Ten dollars was a ton of money, especially for less than an hour's work, and we didn't know what to say except, 'Anything you need. Just let us know. Anytime, anywhere.'

Squalo was smiling. 'That's awesome. I just moved to this neighbourhood so I have a garage full of boxes and files that I need to sort out. Should only take a couple of hours on the weekend. Two weekends at most. Let me know if you guys are free. I can't keep paying these high rates, but I'll find a way to make it up to you.'

It was a strange and an exhilarating experience to be treated respectfully by an adult, and to have our work valued. Karl and I turned up the first weekend and helped to re-organize Squalo's garage, pausing halfway through to drink sodas. Squalo made a big show of taking off his shirt and hanging it on a rack beside the door. 'You guys should take your shirts off too. Your moms will kill me if you show up all sweaty.' I was too self-conscious to take my shirt off, but Karl was still in full flex mode, so he was delighted to show off his physique as he moved one heavy box after another. I almost thought that Squalo was having him move boxes just for the sake of it. But at the end of the day we were each given $15.00 dollars and we returned home feeling like entrepreneurs.

My parents were delighted. 'You see,' my father said, 'these are the opportunities that open up if you take a chance. Good for you, son.' Neither had been to high school and they drank up every detail that I brought home. They were convinced that education was the way out of poverty and disadvantage. I didn't share their certainty, but I couldn't bear to disappoint them. I felt as though I was going to school for them.

Our Saturday part-time jobs continued. Each time was a different task. Sometimes we helped move the furniture in his bedroom, at other times we helped him dig the garden beds. We'd always sit around and share stories and jokes, too, which made us feel grown up. 'What's black and white and read all over?' I asked, and Karl, unexpectedly, answered: 'A Zebra in a blender.'

Squalo doubled over laughing. He was pointing at Karl. 'You,' and then he grabbed Karl in a playful headlock.

'Was that the answer?' Karl mumbled, his head trapped in a tight hold.

'No,' I said feeling a bit jealous at all the attention he was getting. 'A newspaper.'

Squalo let Karl go. 'Clever,' he chuckled. 'I like it.' But there was no enthusiasm in his response. He turned again to Karl. 'You'd better give me your t-shirt. It's covered in dirt. I'll throw it in the washer as we finish up. Wouldn't want your mom angry at me for sending you off looking like a homeless man.'

The following weekend my parents drove us out of town to attend a family funeral. I felt betrayed when I learned that Karl would still work with Squalo without me, but I knew I was just being petty. Still, a voice in my head kept saying, 'You wouldn't have this job if it wasn't for me.'

When I got back to school on Monday, I found Karl sitting alone in the locker room. He had his track suit on and was wearing a heavy sweater over everything despite the heat. He had one sock on his foot and was holding the other absent-mindedly in his hand. 'How's it going?' I asked and sat down next to him. He was nodding but he didn't say anything. 'Did you guys finish cleaning up the garage?'

'Sure,' he said, but he just sat there staring at his sock.

'Everything ok?' I asked.

Karl's head snapped towards me. 'Why wouldn't it be?' he shouted, and then he picked up his things and slammed his locker shut. He headed for the gym, leaving me behind in the silence. I looked at the floor and saw he'd dropped his sock, but I didn't bother to call out.

A few weeks later we heard that Mr. Squalo had been transferred. I went to the main office to get some information. 'Can we still keep in touch with him?' I asked. 'We've been helping him with his garden.' The staff behind the counter grew quiet and looked back and forth between each other.

Mrs. Le Penn, who had first sent me into the principal's office to get the strap on that first day of school, walked to the counter. 'He's not available anymore,' she said sternly. 'He was transferred out of town.' Without saying another word, she closed the metal grill that sectioned off the main counter from the corridor.

Later, when I caught up with Karl, I told him, 'I think Squalo's been sent out of town.'

Karl's head was nodding slowly. 'Good riddance,' he said, and then he walked away.

Thirty-three

CLOSED FOR RENOVATIONS

When I got home from school that night, I was shocked to see an ambulance parked in front of our building, lights blazing like Christmas decorations. I figured one of our customers must have had an accident, so I was confused when my father rushed to intercept me as I moved to look inside the ambulance.

'What's going on?' I asked and then saw my mother on a stretcher inside the vehicle.

A paramedic had his hand on her head as though checking her temperature, but later I realized he was holding her down. She looked disoriented and waved furtively at me when she saw me standing there. 'Dad?'

'Come here son,' and my father led me away from the ambulance towards the store. I watched as the doors closed and it drove away, sirens blaring. 'I need you to stay here,' he said, and pulled me into the building. A small bell that he'd installed above the door, to alert us when customers came in, tinkled gently, and I thought again of Christmas. 'I need you to close up for me. I have to go to the hospital.'

My head was already shaking. 'No way! I'm coming with you.'

'You can't,' he said patiently. 'Kids aren't allowed.'

'What happened? Did she fall?'

'I have to hurry. I'll explain everything when I get back.' He put his hands on my shoulders. 'She's going to be fine. But she has to go away for a while.' He reached into his pocket and pulled out the store keys. 'I'll be back soon, okay, and we can talk. Don't worry.' He hugged me suddenly, the way my mother always did — a bit too hard, as though afraid I might disappear. 'Lock up for me, okay?'

'But it's our busiest night,' I started to argue.

'Put a sign on the door,' he said. 'The customers will understand.'

I looked at the keys in my hand as he left. Holding them gave me a sense of control again, as though I had a role to play. I went in search of a marker and paper and wrote out what I thought was a compelling explanation. As I was preparing to put the sign on the door, though, I saw one of my father's regular clients. I knew him well, and he always bought the same thing, so I figured I would serve him and then lock up. I should have expected that as soon as I turned away to help him, more customers would come in, until I was running from one to the other.

I had grown up in the store, literally, so there was virtually nothing I couldn't handle except mixing the paint. The process to colorize was incredibly complicated, especially with my father's broken-down mixer, so it was the one task I avoided. I ended up cutting a half dozen keys, selling hundreds of dollars of stamps from the small post office my father had installed in one corner of the hardware store, and then, most unexpectedly, a contractor rushed in. He needed gallons of primer. The undercoat was easy for me to sell. There was no mixing, it was a fixed price for the stock, and the customer didn't even want me to pre-shake the cans.

To my amazement he bought out almost our entire supply, and dozens of brushes, pans and rollers. He put $400 in my hand, which in those days was a small fortune. I knew how contractors worked. They always negotiated for a discount, but he wasn't interested. 'Write me a receipt for $500.00,' he said, which I dutifully provided. 'It's a good thing you were open,' he said, 'One of my vans broke down in Oakville, of all places, with all my supply. And I have to finish the job this weekend.'

'Happy to help,' I said, and then he was gone. After he left I found myself standing in the depleted paint section. The customer flow had finally dried up. I heard the little bell ring and the rattle of the rickety door. My father walked over to me. I smelled his reassuring cologne before I actually saw him. 'What are you doing?' he asked. 'Why isn't the door locked?' Then he noticed the wad of bills in my hand. I held it out to him with a stupid expression on my face.

'I tried,' I said honestly. 'But there were too many customers. I couldn't close.'

'Son, that was four hours ago.' He noticed the empty paint display. 'You sold all this?'

'There's also a huge order for wallpaper. I took a fifty-percent deposit. Is that okay? I wasn't sure if that was the right amount.'

We walked over to the broken cash register. It had been smashed repeatedly by opportunistic thieves, but my father had always managed to glue it back together. We rang in the paint sale and then he calculated the total sales for the day. '*Tabarnacle*,' he said. My father never swore, so when he did, I knew something significant had happened. 'This is the biggest single sale day we've had.' He was about to say more but then saw the closure notice I'd prepared. 'Closed for major reconstructive surgery. News at 11. See you tomorrow.' My dad looked at the sign then back at me.

'I wasn't sure what to write,' I said sheepishly. When he didn't answer I asked, 'How's mom?'

I had never seen my father cry before. It happened suddenly. He put his hand to his face and wept! I felt a fear well up inside me that I'd never experienced before. He was my rock, and rocks never crumbled. 'Your mother,' he started to say, and then words left him. 'She's going to be okay.' He had turned away from me, embarrassed to be seen like this. In my family, men didn't cry. They didn't ask for help. They took care of things. That was the code.

'She's going to be fine,' I said, more bravado in my voice then I actually felt. 'She's got you.' His shoulders seemed to crumble when I said this and I felt even more afraid.

'Better put this sign on the door,' he whispered. 'But say we're closed for renovations.'

'But we never close,' I started to argue.

'Just,' and then he stopped speaking. His arms hung down by his side as though they had had their bones removed.

'Okay,' I said, 'of course,' and I went to lock the door.

Thirty-four

HIDDEN

As a gymnast I was used to waking up early, but no matter the time, my father was always up before me. He suffered from severe rheumatoid arthritis and the pain meant that he slept sparingly. On weekends, when most of my friends slept in, my training habits kicked in and I was always out of bed before 6 am. My dad would always be dressed and ready before me. On the morning after my mother went away, I wasn't surprised to find that my father was already up. He was sitting in the kitchen with a cup of coffee, perched in my mother's chair and staring out the window the way she did, lost in thought. I moved to pour myself some orange juice, but I watched him the entire time. I was afraid to interrupt him, as though he was in a private space. But as I sat down, he started to speak.

'So, we could extend this room,' he said. I waited. There was little point in trying to anticipate where he was going or why. 'Your mother always wanted a bigger kitchen. We could knock it off in a weekend. A welcome home present.'

I could hear the old clock ticking into the silence. Finally, I had to ask. 'And when will that be? Coming home from where?'

My father seemed to realize suddenly that I was there. 'You and me. We've built a lot of things together, haven't we?' He smiled, but I could see he was still in a different place. My father was right. He had always included me in his mad schemes. From the day I could hold a hammer I had helped him to fix furniture, to expand the store, and then, perhaps inevitably, to build the apartment above the shop itself. Most of the time we were serving two masters. The first, ever hungry, was the store. We needed more space, and we couldn't expand fast enough to sate its hunger. The other, as different from the first as could be, was my mother.

Although she had been as poor, if not poorer than my dad, she had always aspired to finer things. She had worked as a governess for Mrs. A.'s wealthy family and had come to see how life could be lived. And the shabby, working-class milieu that my dad provided was worlds away from her hopes and dreams. So, he compensated. He built a room above the shop so that she didn't have to tell people that she lived in a hardware store. Quite aside from the fact that it was illegal, so that we had to hide our beds inside display cases, it was also deeply humiliating to her. To me though the display cases remained a refuge; an extraordinary cubby hole that I could access any time I liked. The apartment, when finished, slowly gave birth to a kitchen, and then a bedroom. I slept on the couch until we were able to add another room, four feet by five feet, but a room no less, and all my own. When my father finally built a formal sitting room for her, my mother was overwhelmed. It was really just a square box of a room, but symbolically it was a place of luxury; the only space that didn't have a utilitarian purpose. It even had wall-paper. 'I feel like a lady in here,' she said, sipping tea from a beauti-ful Royal Doulton China cup that Mrs. A. had given her.

'We have four extra feet on the store's roof. If we enclose it that will bring it flush with the living room. One less wall to build. And then she can have her full-sized kitchen.'

'That would be amazing,' I said. We shifted into the living room to check out the weight-bearing wall. The living room was so narrow that we had the couch pushed to one side. My dad's reclin-er was awkwardly placed in the corner of the room to hide a hole he had made in my mother's prized carpet. To her great joy he had splurged and put down a plush olive-green carpet. To her horror he'd cut a hole through it and lowered a ladder into the store. We couldn't afford to heat the store, so he was able to do his paper-work upstairs in comfort, and then climb down when the bell went off announcing that a customer had arrived. 'She'll never notice,' he'd said to me before cutting through the carpet's rich plush.

'I deny any responsibility,' I'd answered, but then I became complicit because he couldn't easily cut through the floor. It was a two-man job. My mother, when she saw the devastation, looked at me accusingly. 'I tried to stop him!' I gushed disloyally.

'You're just like your father,' she said disappointedly. Usually when she said that, it was a good thing. Somehow, with the new intellectual skills I'd acquired in junior high, I had an inkling that this wasn't one of those times.

'When is she coming home?' I asked my dad, and when he didn't answer immediately, I hurriedly added, 'So we can estimate how long the job is going to take.'

He had his hand on the load-bearing wall as though he was try-ing to feel its heartbeat. 'She's pretty sick. She had a nervous break-down. I don't know how long they want to keep her.'

I wasn't sure what that was, but it didn't sound too bad. Many of the British novels I read had characters who suffered from nerv-ous disorders, and it was nothing a handy dose of laudanum couldn't fix. I didn't suggest it because it felt too soon. I would wait for more information. I was about to ask for more details, but someone knocked on the living room window. My dad, at the in-sistence of the fire inspectors, had built a functional fire-escape in the laneway, and a desperate customer had made his way up. He was hammering at the window somewhat frantically.

My father made his way over and forced the window open. 'What do you want?'

The customer gushed in relief. 'I need Draino and a plunger. My toilet is over-flowing. You have to help.'

'We're closed,' I started to say but my dad held up his hand.

'Okay, meet me around the front.' The customer headed back down and my father disappeared into the floor. A few minutes later I heard the bell ring as he opened the shop door. And then, without stop, the bell kept ringing and my father didn't emerge again for another three hours. When he came up and found me sitting on the small couch he came over and put his arm around my shoul-ders.

'Your mother was badly hurt when she was a girl. And she nev-er recovered. We didn't even think we'd be able to have you. So she's having trouble right now.' I looked at him, grateful that he was opening up, but I had no idea what he was telling me. 'She'll be fine, but the doctors want to observe her.'

The days stretched into weeks, and we slowly worked ourselves into a rhythm. I would come home from school and help to prepare dinner, and then we'd take turns serving customers in between bites until closing time. To my mother's dismay I had always insisted on doing my own laundry, so I just included my father's clothes with mine. It was no extra effort at all. After dinner we would watch a television show together or play checkers, but inevitably we got bored and went into the store to work. There was always something to do.

Since the addition to the top of the building had been done in haste, and without a permit, our work was roughshod, and as a result the roof always leaked. So we often spent time replacing the gyprock ceiling, repainting if we could, or up on the roof trying to re-tar and repair. Inside the store we had shelves to build, stock to unpack. At times I would do my homework on one of the display counters while my father did inventory nearby. Each display case had a hinged lid from the days when my father had hidden our beds inside them, safe from prying inspector eyes. I liked to crawl into them every now and then and to lie inside in the silence. The sides we open, the interior hidden only by the stock that we had lining the shelves.

I was doing this one evening, looking out from between the cans of glue, when my father stormed in. To my astonishment, he was followed by Fr. Rémi. It was hard to see properly because of where they were standing, but it was obvious my father was furious, and equally clear that our family priest was trying to calm him down.

'She told him in confidence!' my father shouted, as angry as I'd ever seen him. 'That's the whole point of it, isn't it? The confessional?'

Fr. Rémi tried to console him. 'Nobody broke any confidences,' he said quickly. 'Fr. Rampal just misspoke.'

My father, who had been pacing, suddenly stopped. Fr. Rémi, I could see even from my constrained vantage point, stiffened noticeably. He looked positively frightened. 'Misspoke?' my father seethed. 'Telling her it was her fault that she was raped as a child is not to misspeak? Telling her that she must have led him on is not to misspeak. It's blasphemy. An atrocity.' I heard my father's voice cut out. 'She's locked away in a hospital room right now because she thinks God blames her. That her ten-year-old self was evil. Do you realize…?' He didn't finish his sentence. I had no idea what was going on. I'd never seen my father like this. Fr. Rémi started to walk towards him but my father raised his hand. 'If that priest is still there come Monday,' he began. He stopped and buried his face in his hands. When he pulled them away there was another expression on his face that I'd never seen. I didn't recognize my father.

Fr. Rémi took a couple of steps back. 'He won't be,' he said. 'I promise.' He turned then and left the store. I listened to the slow echo of the bell in the otherwise heavy silence. I could hear water dripping from one of the interminable leaks we could never seal. When I was sure my father had left the room, I climbed out of my hiding spot. I had no idea what to do. My hands were shaking. I could hear my father pacing upstairs. I pulled out the ladder and the caulking gun and tried, futilely, to plug the leaks. But the water kept coming through, no matter what I did, as though the building itself was crying.

Thirty-five

ASH

When my mother finally returned home it was clear that she was different. She had always laughed easily and was quick to hold your hand or hug you in her crushing embrace. She was usually hungry for news about my day, and overly excited about even the smallest occasion. Birthdays and Christmas almost killed her, because she was so excited to see us open our gifts. Knowing that, I would always drag it out, tormenting her playfully. The person who came home that day was preternaturally quiet. I felt like I was greeting a stranger. She actually shook my hand when I held mine out to hold hers.

'Do you want some tea?' I offered and she smiled distantly.

'That would be lovely. Thank you.'

She looked around the kitchen as though she'd never seen it before. She reminded me of a Bernini statue I had seen in a book—of an angel with a broken wing. She eventually found her chair near the window and perched there tentatively, lighting a cigarette with trembling hands. My father, who had been gathering her bags from the car, came in a few beats later and saw me watching her. He put the bags down and moved towards me. He didn't say anything, but the weight of his hand on my shoulder told me to be patient. I watched as the ash of her cigarette grew longer and then moved to catch it before it fell. Too late, it exploded silently across the linoleum floor. Instead, I lifted the cigarette from her fingers so that it didn't burn her. She didn't say a word.

I made her tea and placed it next to her, careful to use her favourite cup. She continued to stare out the window, unaware that I was even in the room. I heard the bell ring and realized that my father had already re-opened the store. So I climbed down the make-shift ladder and went to join him. He seemed to prolong his conversation with the customer, almost as though he didn't want her to leave. Eventually, though, the customer left, and my father was compelled to speak with me. He joined me by the display case. I was half-heartedly unpacking a carton of boxed thumbtacks.

'She's very sick,' he said. 'We have to be patient.'

I stopped stacking the little coloured boxes. 'I don't understand,' I said, and I was surprised how bitterly the words came out. 'I know you think you're protecting me, but not knowing is worse!'

'I know,' he sighed, and he started returning the boxes to the original packing case.

'What are you doing?'

He stopped in confusion. 'I don't know.'

'Who hurt mom?' I asked. 'I heard what you said to Fr. Rémi.'

The look of horror on my father's face terrified me. 'How?' He stopped speaking immediately, his hand on the display case. 'No....'

'I didn't mean to. I was just here.'

He raised his hand and placed it on my cheek. 'What happened to your mother, that was evil. Unforgiveable. But what the priest said to her was just as bad in its own way. Sometimes ignorance can be another kind of evil.' The bell rang then, and I could see the grief etched on my father's face.

'I've got this,' I said, and I moved quickly to the front of the store to make sure the customer didn't see him. My dad was beloved in the neighbourhood, and everyone wanted to chat with him. This wasn't the time.

Luckily it was a quiet Saturday, and my dad, uncharacteristically, shut the store early. When we went up my mother hadn't moved. There were a number of cigarettes burning in a chunky ashtray that I had made her in art class. Ashes had spilled over the lace tablecloth which was pock-marked with little burn marks. My mother was a chain smoker. They had been prescribed to her by her family doctor when she was fifteen as a treatment for her anxiety. But she wasn't smoking them today. She kept lighting the cigarettes and then putting them down, sometimes watching them burn as though she'd never seen such a thing before. Her tea was untouched.

'Do you want some food?' I asked her, to break the silence. Her brow creased, as though she was having difficulty with the concept, and then she shook her head. 'No. Not today dear. I think I may have a nap instead.' With that she rose uncertainly and disappeared into her room.

A few days later I was sitting in the school library by the stacks. I had my notebook open and was unsuccessfully trying to write an essay for my history class. Without meaning to, I kept staring out the window at the bleak winter rain. Sister Anne found me there.

'Hey! How's my favourite singing gymnast.'

'You know more than one?' I quipped half-heartedly, but my tone was flat and her face grew concerned.

'Oh, oh. What's up?' She sat down next to me, leaning forward on her folded arms. 'Come on. You can talk to me. Is Ronald bothering you again?'

I debated what to say, but then, slowly told her what had happened. It took all my willpower not to cry. I knew I was in a public space, and nothing would have been more humiliating. 'Just don't say anything kind,' I finished. 'I can't handle it right now.'

Sister Anne sat next to me for a long time and neither of us spoke. 'You know,' she said at last, 'Your father is right for what he said. And the most important thing for you to do, is to just be there for her. I know it's hard, but even if she doesn't show it, the fact that you are by her side is going to mean the world to her.'

'How do you know?' I asked, and she heard the desperation in my voice.

She took a moment to answer. 'Because women experience a lot of violence. But we're resilient. And having someone you love makes a difference. In fact, it's the most important thing.' I studied her face. 'And faith,' she added, her tone almost apologetic. 'I kind of have to add that in, you know, occupational hazard.' She tapped her crucifix and winked. 'But seriously, it can help to pray.'

'But that priest,' I started to say.

'Is a person, not the faith. Don't lose one because of the other.' She patted my hand and got up to leave. 'I'm glad I have you for a friend,' she said.

'Ditto,' I answered.

When I got home after school, I found my mother seated in her chair again, surrounded by half-smoked cigarettes. I put them out and then took her to her room and tucked her in. When I returned to the kitchen, I tried to wipe away the ash from the tablecloth, but the harder I rubbed, and the more I tried to remove it, the more it stained. It seemed like a metaphor for something, but I couldn't say what.

Thirty-six

CAROUSEL

In the space of a week I felt as though I'd lost two of my closest friends — my mother had retreated into a world I barely understood, and Karl had become combative and angry, lashing out at everyone. His grades began to plummet and he stopped coming to the gym. One of the tough kids from the gymnastics club had even called him out on it — told him that since he was no longer on the team he was fair game. But when he made a move against him Karl lashed out so savagely that the bully ended up in hospital. The principal had to be called and Karl was suspended. I didn't know what was happening.

We were moving towards the last days of school and our final exams were almost finished. I hadn't done as well as I'd hoped because of the situation at home, but it hardly seemed to matter. The world was in freefall. I was sitting alone in the cafeteria, struggling to eat my lunch when Sarah Mohammad sat down next to me. I was surprised to see her, but my heart skipped a beat anyway.

'Hi!' she said.

'Oh, my goodness,' I burst out. 'You look amazing. I haven't seen you in ages.'

She smiled sheepishly. 'Well, we have been avoiding each other. Way too awkward.' I didn't know what to say so I pushed my sandwich towards her. She shook her head. 'What happened to Karl? What's got into him?'

I felt terrible that I didn't have a clue. 'No idea. He just turned up mad one day. A real dickhead. One minute he's your friend, the next he's a psychopath.'

'Guys. Am I right? One minute they're your prom date, the next you're *persona non grata*.'

'Hey!' I said, not quite sure what she'd just said. 'Like, ouch. That's a bit harsh. Under the circumstances. Whatever that means.'

She looked at me with a playful smile on her face, but I wasn't sure if she planned to stab me while I was distracted. You couldn't tell with sophisticated women. 'I'm sorry,' she laughed, 'but you did kind of dump me unceremoniously.'

'Did you, like, study a thesaurus or something? All these fancy words and phrases.'

Sarah leaned over and kissed me. Like she did all those months ago on the bus, but harder and longer. I didn't quite understand how alone I had felt until that moment, and for the first time in my life I actually kissed someone back. With all my heart. My eyes watered and I suddenly felt incredibly stupid. I tried to turn away rather urgently but she caught my face with her hands. 'Hey! Talk to me.' I was shaking my head and trying to move away, and then, suddenly, I kissed her again. I pulled her against me so hard that I felt her heart beating. Or perhaps that was mine. I didn't much care. And then we pulled away, suddenly aware that we were in the cafeteria. We looked frantically around but no one seemed to have noticed.

She took my hand. 'Do you want to catch up? After school maybe? No pressure if you can't.'

'Yes,' I answered, and I thought I sounded way too eager. I debated playing coy, like the cool guys on TV, or the *Playboy* guide I had memorized, but then it occurred to me that I was an unmitigated idiot. The ladies' man I had planned to become had withered on the vine. 'I'll see you after last period?'

'Okay,' she said, and then looked around shyly. She pecked me on the cheek before I could say anything, and then she was gone.

I waited by the main entrance for half an hour past the last class, and it suddenly dawned on me that this was probably an elaborate ruse to get back at me for messing up her graduation plans. I was being stood up. I felt like a complete chump. I zipped up my backpack and headed for the door.

'Hey! Dufous! Where are you going?' I turned to see Sarah running towards me. 'Sorry I was late. Pop quiz. I hate those things. Were you going to dump me again?'

'No!' I lied earnestly, sounding far too defensive. 'I was just going to wait outside. It's kinda stuffy in here.'

She smiled and grabbed my arm. 'Where should we go?'

I was completely stumped. I hadn't thought about the next step. 'How about the park?' I improvised and she nodded.

'Great idea.'

The park was halfway between the school and my house, and we walked, arm in arm, all the way there. I had never had a girlfriend before, and I was surprised how hard it was to walk so close-ly beside someone without tripping over. It looked so easy in the movies. When we got to the park we sat on the rickety carousel and took turns pushing it. All I wanted to do was kiss her again, but I found it wasn't so easy when it wasn't spontaneous. Instead, I asked her about her family, and she slowly revealed that her parents were splitting up. She was freaking out because she didn't know who would take her and if she'd need to change schools again.

Under the weight of her news we stopped pushing the carousel and so we came to a stop. I realized, perhaps overthinking things, that we were either turning in circles, or at a standstill: either way we were going nowhere. It felt strangely familiar.

'Hey!' Sarah said. 'Did you hear what I said?'

I had drifted away for a moment. 'What?'

'Now it's my turn to say ouch!'

'Sorry. But you just made me think about what was going on at my place.'

And then, reluctantly at first, I told her what was happening. I didn't give her any of the details, but I explained that my mom was sick and that everything was uncertain. I felt a weight lift off me just by having someone to confide in. And then we ran out of things to say. So we just sat there as the sky grew darker and the air more chilled.

'I suppose I should head home,' she said at last, and I nodded. We walked to the entrance of the park and paused awkwardly. 'If you don't kiss me goodnight,' she said at last, 'I'm going to perfo-rate your septum.'

'There you go with your thesaurus again,' I laughed, but I kissed her unselfconsciously. My heart was thumping like a bass drum. 'Do I have a septum?' I asked suspiciously.

'See you tomorrow,' she chuckled.

'Yes, you will,' I answered happily. We headed off in different directions, and yet I knew in my heart that we were both dreading our destination. Perhaps a carousel wasn't so bad after all.

Thirty-seven

GRAVITAS

It would be true to say that I had always loved coming home at the end of my day. The store was my playground, and everyone in the neighbourhood knew me, so I felt I had a place — that I belonged. My father was as close to a village elder as you could get, even though he wasn't all that old. People respected him. Many of the first generation Italians and Haitians were indebted to him because he had extended credit to them when no one else would, and then he would usually refuse to collect it. This was one of the major reasons we were struggling. But it meant that people knew my dad was the real deal — that he had their backs. And so, they had ours.

When the big box stores started to open and they began to lure customers away with underpriced products, those my father had helped stuck around. He was an introvert, and he used humour to communicate, but he also had a serious side which no one messed with. Unlike many in the neighbourhood, he refused to lecture people or wax lyrical about whatever was fashionable or objectionable in politics or the church. So when he put his foot down about something, people listened.

'Your dad has gravitas,' a customer said to me once.

'No,' I replied innocently. 'It's arthritis. Rheumatoid arthritis.'

The customer paused for a second and then started to laugh, ruffling my hair. 'You've got your father's quick wit,' he said and walked away, still chuckling. I ran to my room to check the dictionary. It always bugged me when teachers told me to look up the spelling of a word I'd got wrong. If I couldn't spell it, how could I find it? But there it was. 'Gravitas: dignity, seriousness. Someone you respected.' Well okay then.

But things were different now. I dreaded coming home. It was heart-breaking to find my mother sitting alone in her kitchen, a lit cigarette burning nearby, and her hair undone. My mother had always been proud of her looks, and she took great care to 'present herself' as she put it. To see her in a bathrobe was unheard of — terrifying in its own way. It was just as hard to come home and find my father in his dilapidated office, paperwork unfinished, boxes still unpacked. When he served a customer there was no engagement. He had always looked everyone in the eye. Now he rarely raised his head. I had lost both parents that I knew. They had been replaced with automatons.

I was shocked when Mrs. A. arrived, if only because my mother always made a big production of preparing to receive her. She usually baked her friend's favourite treats, and she cleaned the apartment until it sparkled. To see her sitting in her chair and barely moving when Mrs. A. arrived was deeply frightening to me. If Mrs. A. was aware of anything amiss, she didn't show it. She walked over to my mother and took her hands in hers. 'Make us some tea, will you dear?' she said to me, and then, to my mother, 'Come on, let's get you cleaned up.'

With that Mrs. A. led her into her bedroom and got her dressed. She combed her hair, all while singing to her. She had a beautiful voice. An old woman's voice, but you could tell she had been classically trained. I didn't know the song, but she later told me it was 'Shalom Aleichem'. Something about welcoming angels home. Or angels welcoming you home. I couldn't quite remember, but I saw my mother's face when I brought the tea and some of the fear was gone. When she had helped my mother to put on her makeup they moved into the dingy sitting room and sat, as I had seen them before, holding hands in silence. 'It's okay, *habat shelee*. It's okay. We'll get through this. We always do.'

Over the next few weeks Mrs. A. dropped by and helped to settle my mother. Occasionally we would make a meal together, but usually she stayed just an hour or two and helped my mother get dressed or do her make up. They would sit in the kitchen and drink tea together, or in the sitting room smoking, and I gradually heard my mother's voice returning. It wasn't the same, but it was more familiar, and that was something.

One night, as Mrs. A. was preparing to leave, I pulled her aside. My mother had been tucked into bed and my father had gone down to serve a customer. We were open until nine pm on Thursdays and Fridays. 'Mrs. A.,' I said, 'I just wanted to say thanks for helping my mother out.'

Mrs. A. was not a sentimental person in any way. She squared herself in front of me as though she was about to lecture me about not having cleaned my room. But despite her stern manner, her eyes were always smiling, so I was never wary of her the way I was of some of my father's cranky older sisters. 'Your mother,' Mrs. A. said, her voice soft so she wouldn't be overheard, 'Your mother has done the same for me. When I lost my family in a fire, she was there every single day. Came up from Canada to help me. Lost her job and everything because of it. But she wouldn't go home until I could cope on my own. That's what family does. We look after each other.'

'What does *habat shelee* mean?' I wasn't sure if I was pronouncing it correctly.

'It means daughter mine, because that's what she is. My daughter. Maybe not by blood, but in every other way.' Her face got serious. 'Don't thank me again for doing what is right. And you, never leave her side. Even if you travel away, keep her here.' She patted me on my chest, just above my heart. She was so little that she had to stand on the tips of her toes to do it. 'She was told she could never have children. So, you are her miracle. There is nothing in this world that she values more.'

I tried to lighten the mood. 'So, what you're saying is that I'm really, really special, huh?'

Mrs. A. rolled her eyes. 'Oy vey, such a schmuck.' Then she laughed and hugged me. Even though she was as thin as a scarecrow, her arms were like steel. I refused to cry out though. How could I ever face my friends again if I told them that a ninety-year-old woman had crushed me into submission. When she let me go, I noticed that she was crying. I didn't know what schmuck meant, but it clearly moved her to happy tears, so it had to be something good.

'I don't care if you don't want to hear it, I have to say it: thank you. She told me she never got to know her mum, but that it was okay because she had you.' I wanted a big finish, to say something meaningful that would help Mrs. A. see how much I cared for her as well, 'So, you are an even bigger schmuck.'

Mrs. A.'s eyes widened. 'Excuse me?'

'A schmuck. Isn't that what you called me? It means someone you care for, right?'

Mrs. A. started to laugh. 'Yes, indeed, I really, truly do.' She reached up and kissed me awkwardly on the forehead. 'I definitely love you too, you little schmuck.'

Thirty-eight

HOME ECONOMICS

One evening I was speaking with my dad in the living room. The TV was on in the background but neither of us was listening to it. There was a sense of weary exhaustion hovering over my father, but a note of hopefulness too. My mother seemed to be emerging from the shadows, making more appearances, and even, once or twice, visiting my father in the store. It wasn't much, but it was a first step for sure.

I didn't know if the time was right, but I wanted to share my news with my dad. 'So,' I said, a note of disbelief in my voice, 'I have a girlfriend. I think.'

'Well, look at you, a regular Romeo.' We both paused. 'No, poor choice of words. Sorry about that.' He had a playful tone in his voice again which I hadn't heard for some time. 'What's her name?'

'Sarah,' I answered. 'Sarah Mohammed.'

To our surprise my mother came into the room. 'Well, you have to invite her over,' she said, 'Can't have my son dating without having met your parents.'

To say that we were shocked is an understatement. 'Are you sure?' I started to ask.

'Friday. I can cook something nice.' With that she was gone.

My father and I stared at each other nervously. 'Is this a good idea?' I whispered.

He was quiet for a moment. 'Does your friend know a bit about what happened?' I nodded. 'Then why not try? If your mother isn't ready you can go to McDonald's. My treat.'

'Okay,' I agreed, but I couldn't have felt more uncomfortable. It seemed like a terrible plan on every level.

Sarah was equally unsure. 'I haven't even told my parents about you. Worse. My brother doesn't know.'

'Why don't you tell them that I'm a study buddy, and that my parents will be with us the whole time.'

Sarah was looking at me with something approaching disdain. 'Study buddy?'

I shrugged. 'It's a thing. Isn't it?'

'On Planet Dork, maybe.'

I ignored her condescension. 'Friday, if you can. Let me know. My mom will want to over-prepare something, so she'll need some warning.'

'I'll do my best. But I'm not hopeful.'

To my astonishment Sarah returned the next day with permission from her folks. 'I can't believe it, but they said yes.'

'What did you tell them?'

Sarah paused uncomfortably. 'I told them we were ... study buddies!' I gave her the most withering look I could muster, but then I snorted with laughter. She covered her face in mock shame.

'There's more,' she mumbled through her fingertips. 'I told them you were a girlfriend.'

I admit that caught me by surprise. 'Like a lesbian?'

Sarah punched me on the arm! 'No, you idiot! Not like that.'

I rubbed at my arm. She packed quite the punch. 'I am not wearing a dress,' I pouted melodramatically.

'I'm not asking you to,' she started to protest, getting a bit frustrated.

'Although I do have a little chiffon number….'

'Stop! Stop! You've made your point.'

'My legs look great in heels. I'm a gymnast after all.'

'What will it take to shut you up?'

'My calves, they're quite something.'

Sarah rushed towards me, and I thought for certain she was going to punch me again. Instead, she kissed me, though after a half second we both snorted again with laughter. 'Six o'clock?' I nodded and explained what my dad had said. 'Okay, then. I'll be there.'

When it came time for Sarah to meet my parents, I was more convinced than ever that the entire idea was a mistake. We walked to my house together, holding hands, but I was going slower and slower the closer we got.

'Keep this up,' Sarah said at last, 'and we'll be walking backwards.'

'Okay,' I sighed. 'I know. I'm just really nervous. I don't know how she's going to be.'

Sarah stopped and forced me to face her. 'Whatever happens, we'll be okay. If she isn't well, we'll reschedule. There's no pressure, okay?' I stared at her in disbelief. 'What? What's wrong?' she asked, sounding worried for the first time.

'When did you turn thirty?'

'Stop it!'

'I mean it. You're like an old person. In a good way. Like, the most mature person on the planet.'

'Yeah, but I'm also hot.'

'Yes,' I agreed. 'That you are.'

'Well then, what can possibly go wrong?'

That phrase always left me nervous. It was akin to tempting fate. If I was apprehensive before, I was paralytically terrified now. My hand was sweating so much that Sarah diplomatically let go of it, pretending to adjust her skirt. Climbing the long flight of stairs to the apartment above the store seemed interminable. I could hear music, which was a good sign, but I couldn't smell anything. Surely the food was on the stove by now.

When we came in the door my mother was sitting in her chair, a cigarette in hand. She smiled brightly when she saw Sarah.

'Hello! And who might you be?' I realized suddenly that she had completely forgotten we were coming over. My father, mysteriously, was nowhere to be found. I later learned that he had checked on her an hour earlier and that all was well.

'I'm Sarah,' my date announced, and she moved the few feet from the door to the kitchen table before I even had time to process what was happening. I heard my father coming up the ladder. He'd heard my mother's question and he entered the kitchen in a panic just as Sarah grabbed my mother's hand in hers. 'I was in a Home

Economics class with your son, and he asked me to help cook dinner for you tonight.'

My mother was delighted. 'Well, that's unexpected. How exciting. What are you making?' I saw Sarah hesitate just for a moment, and then, with a resolve that simply blew my mind she announced, 'Ratatouille. My specialty.'

'Well, then,' my mother announced, 'I'll go freshen up and leave you to it.'

My mother left the kitchen and the three of us stood awkwardly facing each other.

'Dad, meet Sarah. Sarah, dad.'

My father wrapped his gnarled hands around Sarah's. 'That was very classy,' he said. 'Very gracious indeed. Welcome to our home.'

'Right,' I said, 'Ratatouille. What the heck is that?'

Sarah put her hands on her head. 'Honestly, I don't have the faintest idea.'

'Then why?'

'I don't know! It just … blurted out.'

My father was laughing. 'Okay, then. Spaghetti Bolognese it is. Son, get the onions.'

I turned to do what he asked but first I fixed Sarah with my most disapproving glare. 'Me? In Home Economics? Really? Not cool, girl, not cool.'

Sarah laughed. 'Yeah, well, your dad thinks I'm cool, so there!'

'Hey,' my father called to me playfully, 'don't pick on the genius. Go chop up the onions, servant boy.'

Sarah stuck her tongue out at me in victory. Things weren't going as I'd expected, but perhaps that wasn't entirely a bad thing. Maybe there was hope yet.

Thirty-nine

TWILIGHT

The last day of school was not what I expected. The grade twelve kids had their prom and then their graduation at the local church. Junior high, though, we just kind of fizzled to an end. The last class came and went, and suddenly we were all standing around knowing it was over, but with no celebration. Heck, even a wake would have been something. Instead, we drizzled out of the building into the damp pre-summer air wondering what was next.

Everyone was carrying an overloaded backpack, some even had boxes, because we'd been told to empty our lockers. I had done mine a few days before so at least my hands were free. Karl had come back to school and had managed to finish all his classes. He was arguably the smartest kid in the school so he could pull things together even half-heartedly. We stood facing each other in the little courtyard where James Joyce had been stolen from me, and then recovered. Where Sheriff and his deputies had rescued me in a twilight zone moment. Where, I remembered suddenly, my mother had hugged the life out of me as I entered this foreign world.

'You coming back next year?' I asked, not really knowing what to say.

'Not sure,' Karl answered. 'Thinking I might change schools. Who knows. Right?'

'Yeah,' I said. 'Who knows.'

'Well, see you.'

'Yup.'

Karl turned away and left the schoolyard, and that was that. I didn't see him again. Not that summer, and not the following year. He just disappeared. I was watching him go around the corner out of sight when Sarah came up beside me. Her fingers grabbed mine before I even realized she was there.

'Gotta go,' she whispered urgently. 'But see you at the park later. Soon though I'll introduce you properly to my parents?'

'Sure,' I said, and then I watched her run towards a waiting car. A tall, bearded man was waving at her. I noticed that her brother was sitting in the passenger seat, staring daggers in my direction. 'Great,' I thought. 'There are easier ways to die.' I was about to leave when I heard my name called. I turned to see Sister Anne walking towards me.

'You weren't leaving without saying goodbye, were you?'

I shrugged. 'It doesn't seem real. It's like, everything just ended and then poof. Out you go.'

'Well, I'm glad I caught you. I wanted to give you this.' She put a small plastic pack in my hands. 'It's a rosary. I got this one in the Holy Land so it's quite special to me. I want you to have it.'

'Thank you,' I said. We stood awkwardly for a few moments. 'You know,' I said at last, 'if it hadn't been for you, I don't think I would have made it here.'

'I appreciate you saying that,' she said, 'but you're stronger than you think. And you know what? You did the same for me. This was my first school and having you as a friend made me realize that this was the right path for me.'

'Thanks,' I answered, genuinely grateful. 'I really appreciate that.' It all felt way too sentimental. 'I'm glad that I could help you with your vocation.'

She stared at me with pretend annoyance. 'You had to ruin it, didn't you?' Before I could answer she reached over and hugged me. 'Don't be a stranger. I'll be working at the school through the summer holidays if you find that your brain is atrophying.'

'Will do,' I said, 'I'll look you up when I apostrophe.' And then she, too, was gone.

As I started to leave Mr. Bundengelder came through the door. As soon as he saw me he turned around and ran back inside. No doubt forgot his briefcase, I thought.

I headed towards home but lingered in the park. I was supposed to meet Sarah at five, and I thought it easier to spend three hours waiting then to risk going home. Who knew what might happen? It was a strange feeling to be sitting on the swings alone in an empty park, but as the hour got later, more and more people started to arrive. I moved to one of the benches so that the kids could take over the swings. I watched the odd assortment of parents with their children: single mothers, but a few fathers too, and occasionally a couple, usually with an infant in a pram. Everyone looked happy, but I no longer believed it. I wondered how many of them were hiding secret tragedies.

The air suddenly turned cold, as though rain were imminent. I checked the park to see if there were any places I could hide if it did begin to pour. There was a disused change room halfway across the field, and in a pinch, we could ride out the storm there, but for now I held my ground.

When Sarah found me her eyes were red and puffy. She didn't say anything but wrapped her arms around my neck and sobbed. 'What's wrong? Sarah? What happened?'

Sarah pulled away and slumped onto the park bench. I sat down next to her. 'I'm leaving,' she cried.

'What do you mean? Leaving where?'

Sarah covered her face with her hands. 'My parents. They're splitting up. My mom is forcing me to go back to the states with her.'

'What? When?'

'That's just it. Right away! They'd already made their plans and they were just waiting for school to finish. They didn't even talk to us. I'm going with her and my brother is staying here!'

The only thing that promised to make the long summer ahead of me bearable was the thought of spending time with Sarah. Now my one refuge was gone. 'But don't you have a say?' I asked, knowing how ridiculous I sounded. Sarah just sobbed some more, and I put my hand on her shoulder. I felt my arm suddenly wrenched away and I was thrown onto the grass. When I looked up Sarah's brother was towering above me.

'Don't you dare touch my sister!' he screamed and then reached for Sarah.

'Get off me!' she shrieked and pulled away. 'You're not my dad. Just leave me alone.'

'Do you want me to call dad? To see you like this?'

'Like what? Sitting with my friend? Saying goodbye because we don't have a say in anything?'

I stood up and moved beside Sarah even though her brother loomed aggressively. 'She's not doing anything wrong, man. She's allowed to say goodbye to her friends.'

'Then say goodbye,' he shouted back at me. 'Right now. Or things will get ugly.'

Sarah grabbed my hand quickly. 'Write to me at least?' she said, and her brother grabbed her arm and pulled her away. I watched her disappear just as the rain began to come down. I was halfway home when I realized I didn't have her address. I didn't even have her phone number. I knew then and there that I would never see her again.

Later that evening my mother put a bowl of soup in front of me for dinner. I could see that she had forgotten to heat it up, but I wasn't going to say anything.

'I'm going to lie down now,' she said, and started to walk away. She stopped in the doorway. 'That girlfriend of yours? When did you say she was coming over for dinner?'

'She's not coming,' I answered, and I felt my chest tighten. 'She couldn't make it after all.'

'Oh, that's too bad,' she said. 'Another time perhaps. I'll make something special.'

And then, without realizing it, she turned the light off and left the room. I sat in the dark, holding the spoon, fighting the urge to scream. But who would hear, I thought. Would anybody even hear?

Forty

EPILOGUE

It is a falsehood to claim that youth is wasted on the young. It is in fact revisited and re-prosecuted throughout one's life, a template upon which we tweak and tug, draft and redraft the actions of our future selves. The first loves never die. They are relived, reinvented, regretted and reborn. We remember loved ones and other passions through the frame of an imperfect lens, that sets the stage for disappointments yet to come. If we are lucky then humility is born from the fragility of failure, and we move more cautiously towards a stronger self. In the end, we are left with the fabric of a life well-lived, partially fulfilled, or completely unimagined. Perhaps that is all we can demand of fate: that we remember, and be remembered by, the ghosts that shaped us and possibly set us free. It is, one must hope, enough.

Afterword

ALL THINGS BEING EQUAL

It is hard to believe that my first novel, *Flying in Silence*, appeared some twenty-five years ago. It told the story of a hapless young man trapped between languages, cultures and family tragedies. To be honest, I thought I had said all I needed to say about that distant time. So, I was quite surprised when *A Space Between* appeared seemingly out of thin air. Clearly, I told myself, I had more to say about this subject than I thought. But *A Space Between* is not so much a sequel as an 'equal.' It retraces some of the same territory, but through a different lens, and even contradicting some of the earlier trajectories.

While it is also clearly auto-biographical in a great many ways, it is also a novel which exaggerates, invents and transforms the past, hopefully in comic and unexpected ways. It is not the role of a novelist to be true to the past — merely honest about the stories and their impact on one's understanding. Where I grew up closely connected to friends in the Jewish faith, for example, for the purposes of the comedy and the tragedy, my character here is oblivious to that story. This was necessary in order to speak about the way we can be blind to truth, to experience, even when we are in the midst of it.

While not fully auto-biographical, much is true about the struggles, the goodness of the people, even the at-times tragic violence — verbal and physical — that marked our lives back then. These violences shape us, indirectly compel us to find our voice, and set us on a path to completion, whatever that may mean or look like. As such, and as I so often say with all of my writing, I can only hope this finds a sympathetic audience.

WHAT THE CRITICS SAID ABOUT
FLYING IN SILENCE

Ian McFarlane, *Canberra Sunday Times*

"He's written such a sensitive and wonderfully evocative piece about growing up in Montreal it's hard to believe the front cover disclaimer that 'although written in the autobiographical voice it is a work of fiction'. But then, self-revelation has always been an important facet of good writing... This is a rites of passage story, trapped between two languages... The narrator watches and waits, eventually finding another world, made larger by the memory of his parents."

Liam Davison, *The Sydney Morning Herald*

"Most first novels are thinly disguised autobiographies. Gerry Turcotte's is no exception except that he does it better than most. Not because he has lived a particularly exciting life (his narrative intersects with no major world events) but because he has an eye for telling detail and a poet's ear for language."

Fiona Capp, *The Age* (Melbourne), 'Pick of the Week'

"Written in the first person and constructed around distilled moments of recollection, this is a novel with the painful immediacy and emotional authenticity of a memoir."

Michelle Grattan and Mark Rubbo

The Age Book of the Year shortlist

"When we agreed to be judges it was with a secret hope that we would discover a writer who was unknown to us and a marvelous book we weren't aware of. Gerry Turcotte's *Flying in Silence* is such a work. In this novel, the narrator tries to piece together the fragments of his childhood in Montreal and understand the sadness of his parents; his French working-class father, forever beginning projects he would never finish; his English mother aspiring to a grander life, sliding into depression. Turcotte's narrator inhabits an in-between world, both culturally and linguistically, that is both confusing and comical, and partly explains the tensions in his family... Above all *Flying in Silence* is a beautifully crafted novel about growing up, full of humour, warmth and a strangely comfortable melancholy. It's Turcotte's first work of fiction and an exciting find."

OTHER BOOKS BY GERRY TURCOTTE

Creative Works

The Ghost Wilderness and other plays

Flying in Silence (Shortlisted for *The Age* Book of the Year)

Ridgedon's Fowl: a novel

Border Crossings: Words & Images

Winterlude (poems)

Neighbourhood of Memory (poems)

hauntings: the Varuna poems

Academic Works

The Oxford History of the Novel in Australia, Canada, New Zealand & the South Pacific (with P. Sharrad & C.A. Howells)

Peripheral Fear: Transformations of the Gothic in Canadian and Australian Fiction

Unsettled Remains: The Postcolonial Gothic in Canada (with C. Sugars) (Shortlisted for the Gabrielle Roy Prize for Literary Criticism)

Literary and Social Diasporas: An Italian-Australia Perspective (with G. Rando)

Canada–Australia: 1895–1995: Towards a Second Century of Partnership (with L. Foster and K. Burridge)

The Sum of All Things: Essays Old and New

One Last Thing: Reflections on Hope and Resilience

Big Things: Ordinary Thoughts in Extraordinary Times

Small Things: Reflections on Faith and Hope

Compr(om)ising Post/colonialism(s): Challenging Narratives and Practices (with G. Ratcliffe)

Jack Davis: the Maker of History

Masks, Tapestries, Autobiographies

Writers in Action: The Writer's Choice Evenings